Good luck with the

C000155969

Terror
Byte

J. R. Park

Other books by J. R. Park:

PUNCH
UPON WAKING

Further books by the Sinister Horror Company:

BURNING HOUSE – Daniel Marc Chant
CLASS THREE – Duncan P. Bradshaw
MALDICION - Daniel Marc Chant

Visit JRPark.co.uk and SinisterHorrorCompany.com for further
information on these and other coming titles.

TERROR BYTE

J.R. PARK

SINISTER
HORROR
COMPANY

Terror Byte
Second edition

First Published in 2014
This edition 2015

Cover design and chapter cover skull design by Vincent Hunt
www.jesterdiablo.blogsport.co.uk
Twitter: @jesterdiablo

ISBN-13: 978-0-9932793-1-7

JRPark.co.uk

ACKNOWLEDGEMENTS

I'd like to thank Stuart Park, Jess Spurway & Daryl Mazelin for taking the time to read the rough drafts of my first work and giving me greatly valued feedback. Without your comments and support this story may still be rattling around in my head.

Thanks also goes to Danielle Robinson for suffering many late night phone calls to be quizzed about police protocol and equipment.
Most of which I probably got completely wrong.

For my brothers Gav and Stu. You always knew I was going to write a book. I should have believed you.

J. R. Park

Mel.

Matt looked at the word written on the flash drive he idly flipped between his fingers. He'd found the small piece of hardware on the ground earlier in the day during the light relief that was his lunch break. It had been floating down a small stream created by the blocked drainage system and torrential rain, just outside his office building.

It was a horrible day outside, made worse due to it being a Monday. His hangover had been raging. A bitter reminder of the nagging doubt he ignored when he went to the pub *for one* yesterday afternoon.

He had gone out with Tim and despite them both drinking equally and no doubt being equally hung over, unlike Matt, Tim had seemed surprisingly chipper throughout Monday morning. It became apparent why his friend was so happy when they ventured out on their lunch break to get some food.

'She is gagging for it mate!' beamed Tim, his smile facing directly into the heavy rainfall, defying its misery with an expression of mischievous glee.

Matt shook his head in disbelief, 'Jayne Amble is up for it with you?'

'Don't sound surprised my friend,' said Tim talking through the pieces of burger he was chewing. 'We've been flirting via email for weeks and we kissed last Friday, just before her boyfriend came to meet us all. She wants it.'

'You should be careful, Tim.'

'You're right I should and that's why I need you to do me a little favour...'

That *little favour* was the reason why Matt was currently keeping an eye on a door. The door led to the post room, which was a small room just off the main workspace of the office. Although it could be better described as a cupboard masquerading as a room. It was a place where all the post was collected up, franked, and sent out each day at twelve.

Tim knew that the room would rarely be used after one o'clock and conveniently his best mate Matt sat directly opposite it with a good view of anyone that might be approaching. He was also aware of how thick and heavy the door to the post room was; thick enough to block sound, making it perfect for today's plan.

Mel.

The words were all that were left from the original insignia of *Memory Inc*, once printed on the plastic casing. The flash drive had seen better days but had survived the battering of the storm outside. Matt was pleased to have found it and from what he could make out by the printed markings that hadn't worn away it was 300 GB in size. A good find indeed.

Tim and Jayne had already slipped inside the post room.

A few minutes ago Tim had sent Matt an email saying, 'It's on.'

Instinctively Matt had looked over to Jayne and saw her casually and calmly stand up. She always looked beautiful and today was no exception. Her long, blonde hair flowed down her neck, over her shoulders and rested, sensually, by her breasts that were barely contained within the white blouse she wore. Jayne moved delicately and confidently on her heels across the room and Matt couldn't help but watch the perfect curves of her bottom in her grey pencil skirt as she walked past his desk. His eyes traced her slender legs down towards her shoes. He loved it when she wore those stilettos. He noticed her give Tim a sly wink, then she disappeared into the post room. The door closed gently behind her.

Approximately twenty seconds later Tim stood up, a little more awkwardly than Jayne had managed. His excitement and nerves of the situation were showing, but only to Matt, only because he knew what was going on. Tim hit his thigh against the desk as he rose from his chair causing a loud bang. The whole office stopped and looked at him. He sheepishly made an apology and, trying to ignore the pain, he hobbled over to Matt's desk. By the time he'd reached his friend the disruption had been forgotten and everybody continued about their business.

'Thanks buddy,' Tim whispered to Matt as he made his way to the post room, his penis already swollen with anticipation and desire.

The post room was a confined space so the moment Tim walked in he found himself in a clinch with Jayne. Their arms wrapped around each other as their lips met in a passionate kiss and an explosion of lust. One of his hands firmly held the back of her head whilst their tongues explored each other's mouths. His other hand slid down her well-formed buttocks and clenched her thigh. As he did so he could feel the edge of a stocking under her pencil skirt. Excited by the new discovery Tim pushed Jayne against the wall. She gasped as his fingers slipped under her already damp underwear and found her moist, excited pussy. His fingers continued to probe and easily made their way into her wet, velvet-like vagina. He began to massage her clit, causing her legs to shake and her pelvis to grind against his hand. Jayne bit his earlobe seductively and let out a gentle moan. She raised one thigh and pulled his crotch towards hers. Reaching down to his groin Jayne could feel his hard cock throbbing through his suit trousers

'I want you,' she groaned in lustful passion as his lips explored her neck, sending waves of pleasure through her body.

Jayne began to rub the bulge in Tim's trousers and simultaneously they began to pull at each other's clothes.

Tim unbuttoned Jayne's blouse, sliding her breasts out from her bra and licking her exposed nipples.

They quickly grew hard under his careful attention and she moaned again as electric bolts of ecstasy coursed through her.

'Give me your cock,' Jayne whispered in his ear as she unzipped his trousers, reached in and freed his achingly hard penis.

She pulled her underwear to one side and massaged her clit with the end of his throbbing helmet. Rubbing it round and round her pulsating pussy she began to tease her vaginal lips apart. The wetter she got the harder she thrusted, biting her lip in a vain attempt to keep her orgasmic groans from being heard. After a few moments of teasing herself in this way she grabbed Tim's ass and thrust him forward, forcing his huge cock to fill every inch of her eager pussy. He penetrated her hard and deep. Sensing that she was losing control, Tim put a hand over her mouth and Jayne began to moan violently with pleasure as their rhythm increased.

'You wouldn't dare. I bet it's stacked with porn anyway!'

Matt remembered what Tim had said to him on their lunch break when he found the flash drive floating on its way to the storm drains.

Tim and Jayne had been in the post room for a while. Lucky bastard. Tim always got the girls, always had the action and excitement. Surely it should be Matt's turn to get lucky. Tim always seemed so willing to take the risk, would Matt do the same? He had always been a careful person, he didn't want to rock the boat too much; kept his head down and got on with things. Maybe that was the problem. Maybe he needed to be a bit more like Tim. Matt was such a cautious person. So cautious he wouldn't even have the balls to put the flash drive he found into a computer to find out what was on it.

The thought sounded ridiculous as it passed through Matt's mind. Not even brave enough to load up a flash drive? A stupid memory stick found in the street. What's the worst that could happen? The office computer network was loaded up with so many anti-virus programs and firewalls that you needed permission just to view news websites.

Tim was in the post room fucking a girl's brains out whilst he was standing guard. Was he always going to spend his life standing guard whilst others had all the fun?

Oh to hell with it, Matt thought and inserted the flash drive into his computer.

It was a minor act of rebellion, but the rash action sent adrenaline through his body and his pulse throbbed in his throat. Licking his suddenly dry lips he looked over his shoulder. No one had seen him. He looked back at the computer screen and clicked on the mouse. The computer displayed a removable drive icon with the name *Memory Inc.* Nervously he clicked on it. What could be contained within the potential treasure he'd discovered?

His mood was a little deflated to find it only had one file in its memory. It wasn't exactly the bounty he was hoping for. The file was simply the image of a plain document with a title underneath: *Execute.*

Matt hovered the mouse cursor over the icon and double clicked.

He closed his eyes and turned his head to the

side as if shielding himself from what he'd just done.

After a few moments he turned back to the monitor and cautiously opened his eyes. As he did so he found his screen just as he'd left it.

Nothing had happened.

Incensed with a feeling of anger that his first foray into bold action had been fruitless, Matt went to pull the flash drive from the computer when a message box appeared on his screen. The box simply said *Execute?* with an *OK* button underneath. Now feeling a little victorious that his pursuits were going somewhere he boldly clicked *OK*, his curiosity overriding the fear he'd previously had.

Another box appeared on the computer screen.

Activating.........it displayed, then: *Setting Targets*......

That doesn't sound good, thought Matt as suddenly his fear returned. He began to hit the Escape button on his keyboard, desperate to halt the program he had set running. But it didn't stop.

'Oh shit,' exclaimed Tony Bevis sitting two desks from Matt. 'Has anyone else got problems with the phones?'

'Yep,' called out Hilary Peel from across the office.

'Looks like the emails have stopped working too. Someone had better call IT,' came another voice.

Matt took hold of the flash drive and pulled out his computer, hoping to halt the program as a nauseous feeling grew in his stomach. Was he responsible for this systems failures?

Another message appeared on his screen:

Location determined. His computer screen started to flicker and crackle. He looked around and saw the visual disruption wasn't just happening to his monitor, but to everyone else's as well.

'What the hell is that?' screamed Sandy as she pointed at the wall mounted TV, usually displaying the twenty-four hour news channel.

The TV picture had gone, replaced by a mass of static. But this was no random blur of pixels. The static had formed into the shape of a primitively drawn skull. Its form, made of ever-pulsating black and white dots, shook on the display, refusing to stay permanently in one position. It shrank and grew with size, its proportions fluidly distorting, giving the illusion that its strange, alien eyes were searching the room whilst its electrically generated mouth seemed to widen with an evil intensity.

Around the office the computer screens began to blink and flicker, at first in slow and seemingly random sequences but quickly they began to unify. The speed of the flashes increased, faster and faster, until they became a pulsating strobe of intense brightness. At that very moment the lights in the office failed. The dull weather outside gave little illumination through the windows as the freakish light show within continued.

Fascinated by the strobing computers they all looked, hypnotised by the screens, whilst wondering what was going on. Without warning Tony started to shake and convulse in his chair. His eyes rolled to the back of his head and drool foamed from his mouth like a rabid dog. He was quickly joined by others; Sandy, Joe. They began to fit violently too, falling from their chairs and continuing their seizures on the floor.

Panic set in and the others began to run from their desks, some to their fitting colleagues to help, others attempting to escape these strange events.

Matt broke his gaze from the screen and ran to Tony's aid. He crouched beside his fitting colleague and tried to recount the first aid training he'd completed a few years ago, but his mind was blank, consumed with fear and confusion. He held Tony by the shoulders and tried to stop him from thrashing around.

'Come on Tone, calm down,' he pleaded.

Suddenly Tony went limp.

Placing the side of his face close to his workmate's lips, Matt could not feel any breath against his cheek. He opened up the dying man's mouth and began to perform the kiss of life.

It was as he breathed a lungful of warm air into Tony's corpse that a huge, searing flash burst from all the screens, much brighter than any of the strobes previously. He looked up and watched as people he'd been talking to only minutes before dropped to the floor, dead; their lifeless eyes bleeding from their sockets, their pupils glazed and cloudy. Others stumbled around as if in the dark, grasping wildly at the air and crashing into chairs and desks. The flash had been devastating in its ferocious intensity; killing some out right, blinding those that had survived.

Matt tried to keep his thoughts rational amid a scene of panic, screaming and death. He tried to think who to help first when a high-pitched whine started to emanate from the computers. At first he could barely hear it and wondered if it was just the ringing in his ears from the cries of the blind, but as it increased in frequency and intensity he began to feel sick and dizzy. The pitch increased until it seemed to stop being a sound at all and became a feeling affecting his whole body. Matt stumbled to his feet, staggering like a drunk at closing time as he discovered the sound was causing havoc with his balance. Desperately he tried to maintain co ordination whilst his head seemed to fill with the noise. He felt it behind his eyes as his head throbbed in pain and his stomach began to convulse, making unsettled burbling sounds. He had to get out and find help. He ran, clumsily to the door and fell towards it. The high-pitched noise continued, as he felt a violent jerk in his gut causing him to vomit. Bile and semi digested food streamed from his mouth and nose, showering his legs as he lay against the door. The sharp smell of stomach acid hung in his nose stinging his nasal cavities. He pulled himself to his feet using the door handle then wildly shook it, but his exit would not open. He manically pressed the electronic release, slapping the green plastic button marked *open*, but again the door stayed firmly in place, blocking his escape.

Matt screamed in agony as his head continued to throb. Realising he had no way out he crumpled to his knees crying in the resolution that he had met his end. Amid his anguish he felt his ears turn warm and wet, the noise seemed to stop, but he knew it hadn't. Putting his hand to his ear he felt the warm, sticky texture of blood that poured from his burst eardrums. He erupted into tears as he collapsed to the floor, bleeding to death, only inches from escape.

The flashing and noise stopped as suddenly as it had begun. Bodies lay strewn around the office with blood and vomit trickling from their eyes, nose, ears and mouths. The door to the post room slowly creaked open and the horrified faces of Jayne and Tim surveyed the scenes of slaughter in front of them.

'What the hell?' whispered Tim, shaking and white with fear.

They stepped through the dead bodies and puddles of blood. Their feet were unsteady on the slippery surface, made so hazardous by the bodily fluids that puddled and pooled between the corpses.

'We've got to get out of here,' Jayne whispered, 'come on.'

They held hands and picked their way through the putrid carnage to the door.

'Help me,' Jayne urged Tim for assistance as she grabbed the body blocking the exit and tried to move it.

'Oh my God it's Matt,' cried Tim. He looked at the fear stricken features on the face of his best friend who'd died merely a matter of minutes ago.

'Shhhh. Come on,' Jayne reassured him trying to keep their focus on what was the most important task at hand.

Together they heaved the dead weight of Matt's bleeding corpse from the exit and pressed the electronic release button. The door opened.

They ran through the exit, but feeling a hand grip her ankle, Jayne fell forward with a shriek. Turning round she saw Matt, just holding on to life with as much determined effort as he held on to her. Her instant reaction was not of pity but to fight him off, to get out of this room thick with death. She instinctively kicked out hard and struck him against his head. Her stiletto, one Matt had previously admired so much, smashed into his face at a violent velocity. The long pointed heel was driven into his eye, puncturing the fragile tissue of the eyeball and pushing it back into his skull. His grip instantly relaxed and, wiggling her footwear free from his eye socket, Jayne stood to her feet.

'I'm not hanging round to find out what did this, come on!' said Jayne as she opened the lift door and beckoned Tim in.

They entered the lift and pressed the button marked G for the ground floor and to safety. The lift started to move then abruptly stopped, shuddering as it came to its sudden halt. The lights began to flicker sporadically and a buzzing sound of intense electrical current hummed from the fittings. Tim pressed the alarm button but neither of them could hear any sound to signal their predicament. He pressed it again, and again.

'Come on!' he shouted. 'Come on!'
The alarm still didn't ring but, without warning, the speakers began to emit the sound of static. The lift began to shake and then suddenly it dropped. Faster and faster they felt the lift fall as it sped past each floor. It shook and shuddered as it bounced off the sides of the shaft on its free fall to the bottom. Tim and Jayne turned to each other with terror in their eyes. They sensed the lift was falling and knew what was coming. Together they embraced. Holding each other tightly they closed their eyes tighter still as the lift car hurtled toward the ground and their certain death.

2

J. R. Park

The Areas building stood tall in the fashionable and cosmopolitan sector of the city. It was surrounded by beautiful old trade buildings that had long been converted into banks. Exquisite sculptures of angels and animals adorned these structures as they overlooked busy roads full of business women and men that never stopped chasing the next sale. In contrast to the surrounding designs of antiquated splendor the Areas building was a twelve storey concrete block. But what it lacked in outside grandeur it made up for in popularity. The rent was cheap and the area was good which meant each floor was full; rented out to separate companies desperate to give themselves a business edge with the prestigious address the building provided.

A security guard stood outside the main entrance letting the rain soak him. As he felt the rain splash against his face he hoped it would wash away the repulsive sight of what he had glimpsed earlier. Nothing could have prepared him for what he saw when he first heard a loud metallic crash from one of the lifts and prised apart the two sliding doors. That had happened yesterday but he had been not been allowed to forget the image. He had been held overnight for questioning and for nearly twelve hours he'd been asked to repeat what he had done and what he had seen, again and again. He wanted to sleep and forget. He looked back through the glass doors of the entrance and studied the lift lobby. He hoped the police would allow him to go home soon.

The floor of the lift car was awash with blood and broken bone. Pieces of flesh were splattered up the walls like crimson graffiti and slowly dripped from the ceiling. The impact had been so hard it had snapped bones, torn flesh and turned its unfortunate occupants into an unrecognisable pool. The twisted metal box of the lift car had been both their executioner and their tomb.

As they hit the ground in a fearful and desperate embrace Tim's face had smashed into the top of Jayne's head. The resilience of her skull had caved his face in, obliterating his nose to nothing more than a gaping hole and knocking his teeth out leaving some imbedded deep into Jayne's cranium. Their limbs had been twisted, broken and bent round to such unnatural degrees that they stopped looking human. So much so that when the police had first arrived on the scene they were unsure just how many people had met their grizzly end in this doomed lift car.

'Lucky buggers,' the remark came from a grey haired man in a police uniform. He was taking photos of the inside of the car, stopping between each photo to ponder. As he did so he twisted the corner of his moustache with his thumb and index finger.

Around him the hallway was a hive of activity. Blue lights flashed through the windows, emitted from the swarm of police cars parked outside.

He turned to face a stocky, well built detective. The detective was no taller than 5'9" but was almost as wide. He carried a certain amount of fat on his frame that rounded his belly and hid the separation of his head from his shoulders, but that also concealed a large bulk of well earned and well fought for muscle. He had thick, powerful hands, his hair was black with flecks of grey and his face was hardened with age and experience. Standing in the lift lobby he wore a brown suit, but somehow managed to make it look scruffy, like he'd slept in it for the last week. Although his weary and tired expression put paid to any theory that he might have actually had some rest in the last seven days or so.

'Lucky buggers? How do you think that, Gilbert?' the stocky detective asked the police photographer, scratching his strong, stubbly chin and surveying the blooded lift car.

'These two, and we're pretty sure it's only two, would have died almost immediately. As soon as the car hit the ground, bang, they'd have been dead. It's the ones upstairs I feel sorry for Norton.'

'What happened upstairs?' Norton asked, still scratching his chin and wondering what horrors were going to be worse than the sight in front of him. He'd seen a lot in his long career in the police force but that didn't make seeing these sights any easier.

'Well at first we thought it was some kind of

disease or chemical terrorist attack. But we've had this place shut down all night, had the bio-hazard unit in. Plastic tunnels, gas masks and chem suits; the lot! But they found nothing. Not a trace of anything. The building has been given the okay otherwise we wouldn't be standing here now.' Gilbert stopped taking photos and waved the detective to follow him, 'Come on up, I'll show you.'

They both got into another lift car and Gilbert pressed the button marked 6. The car shuddered then began its climb; the two continued to talk.

'Is this thing safe?' Norton tapped the lift with his fist as he asked.

'Completely,' Gilbert assured him, 'we've had a full engineer and systems check on the building. This lift is as sound as any other.'

'That's not very comforting,' Norton remarked shaking his head.

'Aside from the bodies on the ground floor all the action happened on the sixth floor,' Gilbert explained, 'and only the sixth floor.'

'So why did you think it was chemical or disease related?' Norton queried.

'The mess of them all, Norton,' a look of horror spread across Gilbert's face. 'I've seen a lot of bad shit, but this! So much awful mess! Horrific! The whole office was dead, eyes were burnt out, tongues bitten off, people crushed in stampedes. And the vomit and crap that these people excreted as they died.'

They exited the lift and walked across the lobby to the office door.

'It's right through here,' explained Gilbert.

He led Norton through a door to reveal the horror that he was talking about.

'Good God!' exclaimed Norton.

As Gilbert had described, a massacre lay in front of his eyes. Bodies strewn everywhere, crumpled where they fell. Furniture tipped over, computer screens smashed. The place was a riot zone. The smell caused Norton's stomach to tighten and he felt bile shoot up his throat. He reached into his pocket and pulled out a white handkerchief, placing it over his mouth to filter the air he was breathing.

'Pretty rough huh? You'll get used to it. Hold on,' Gilbert said as he put his arm out to stop Norton walking forward into the crime scene.

Norton looked up to a see a large camera on a mechanical arm being operated by a police officer. The camera emitted a red light that swept over the room.

Gilbert explained, 'A wonderful piece of technology. This thing will scan and make a computer simulation of every detail of the scene. We can then pick over the whole thing at our leisure in the lab. Fascinating stuff. It can make scans right down to particle level. It really is amazing what computers can do now-a-days.'

Norton looked at the machine with a sense of bewilderment.

'No substitute for getting your hands dirty,' he muttered.

'There'll be plenty of that. As soon as the scan has finished, clean up will commence. There'll be plenty of dirty hands then,' Gilbert quipped, 'should all be done today. Then the world can carry on its business.'

'Leaving us to pick up the shitty end of the stick,' Norton cut in.

'Well, yes,' Gilbert retorted matter-of-factly.

The scanning machine stopped moving and its red light faded as it reached the end of the recording process. Norton's attention snapped back from the state of the art policing technology and turned itself to the foul stench and homicide at hand.

'So what happened here?' he puzzled. 'The place is a mess with obvious signs of struggle. Any witnesses? What do the cameras show?'

'Well,' said Gilbert, in a tone that suggested bad news, 'the security on the front desk report no unauthorized entry. The whole mess was only discovered after the lift car hit the ground. Security evacuated the building and did a sweep. Unlucky buggers.'

'And the camera footage?' asked Norton pointing to a security camera in the corner of the room. It was attached to the wall, close to the ceiling, and overlooked the whole office.

'Nothing. The cameras…uh…stopped working,' came Gilbert's response.

'Stopped working?' Norton could barely believe what he was hearing. 'All of them? There's one in each corner!'

'Well…yes,' Gilbert spoke like he agreed with the incredulous mood in which the questions were asked, 'some sort of temporary malfunction. But they seem to be working fine now.'

'That's insane,' muttered Norton as his big frame walked about the office.

Mel.

Norton stopped in his tracks and looked down at a memory stick lying on a blood soaked desk. He read the scratched and scuffed letters on its casing. His face changed from an expression of outward disgust to one of inward horror.

He turned and headed to the exit.

'It's like I'm being haunted,' he muttered.

'What?' Gilbert called after him.

'Doesn't matter,' came Norton's reply as he walked back to the lift.

3

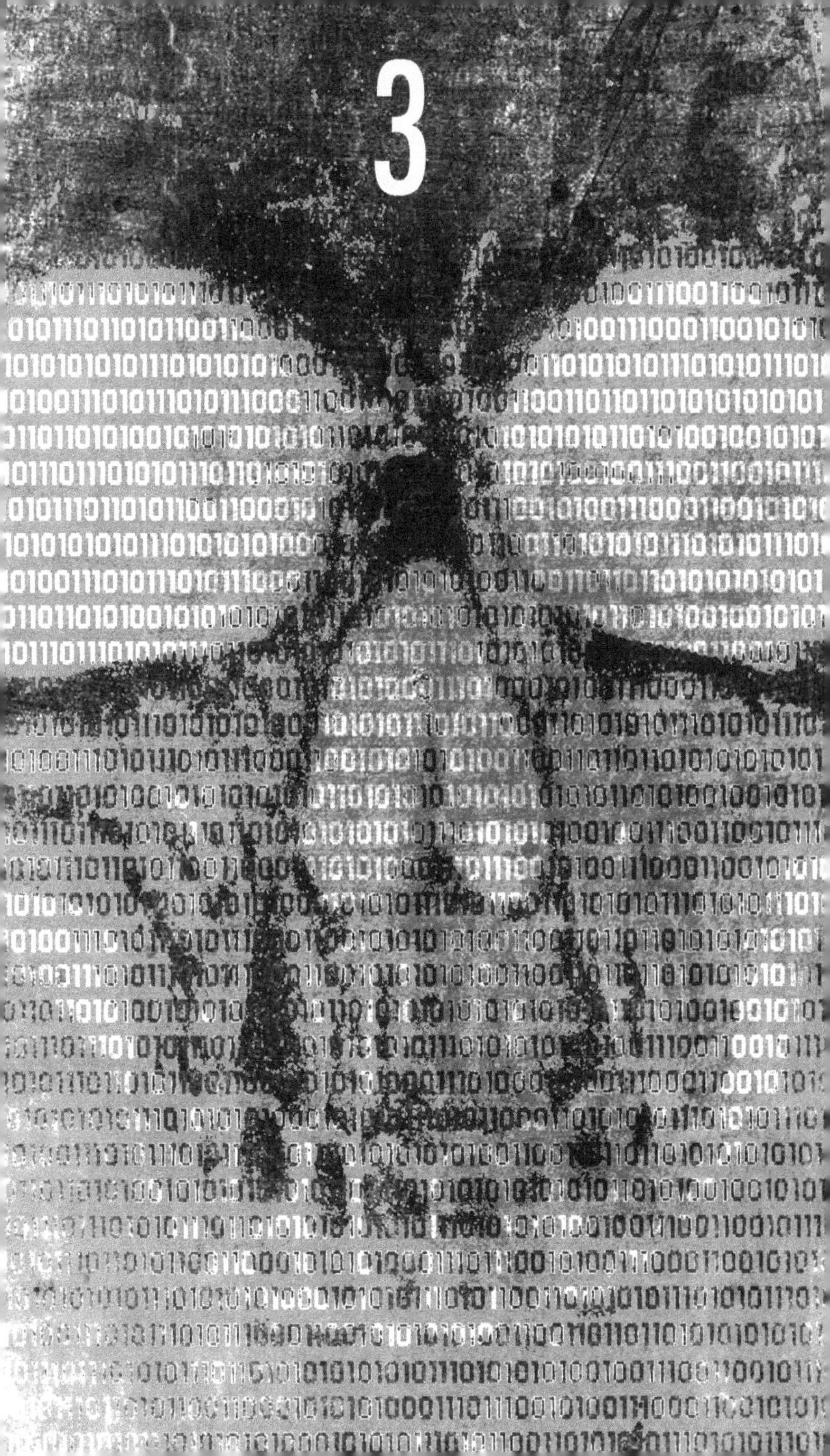

J. R. Park

The police station was an archaic building; a light stone dome with tall, chipped pillars on either corner, making it resemble a Roman relic, a monument to law enforcement and budget cuts. Its tattered and dilapidated state made it nearly fit in with the surroundings, for it was positioned on the edge of the industrial sector of the city. Surrounding it were old factories, some used, some long since abandoned. Chimneys puffed plumes of smoke and the smell of sulfur hung in the air. If it hadn't been raining so hard the wind would have been throwing paper and litter around like suburban tumbleweeds; but as the rain lashed down the rubbish was floating along makeshift rivers, the drains blocked a long time ago and neglected for even longer.

Police Constable Andrews stood outside nervously checking the shine of his shoes and wondered if he should have made so much effort. He had just been enlisted to this station and at first was excited about the opportunity but now he was left wondering who he had upset.

'PC Andrews,' his worried meditations were broken by the voice of a female officer. She walked towards him and held out her hand. 'I'm Sergeant Robinson, pleased to meet you.'

Sergeant Robinson smiled at him, the hat of her uniform framed a face that held a welcoming softness, but behind her big, friendly, green eyes he could sense the flickering of a fire that was not to be reckoned with. Andrews extended his hand and they shook with a firm grip.

'Pleased to meet you,' he said, shouting to be heard over the storm.

'Welcome to your first day. Let's get out of the rain. I'll show you around,' Sergeant Robinson said as she turned and walked back towards the entrance of the station.

Andrews followed her inside.

'It may not look like much, but we work hard. I'm sure you'll have heard of our reputation,' she explained as they walked through the entrance and out of the storm. 'I'm not one to brag but we have a great team and get great results.'

The inside of the station was just as run down and grim as the outside. Paint was peeling off the walls, patches of damp festered in the corners and chunks of plaster were missing as if punched out, leaving mementos of the violent forays that had taken place over the years. The holes held the gravitas of a warning to anyone that entered that this was a force demanding respect. Before them was a large plastic screen manned by a tired looking Police Officer, his hair was a sandy color, his eyebrows big and bushy and bags sunk heavy under his eyes. A strange looking gentleman had just finished talking to him and was making his way out of the station. He was a short, middle-aged, man and completely bald. His skin was tanned and hardened by the sun whilst his bottom lip hung in an uncontrolled and peculiar way.

'Hello Mr Light,' said Sergeant Robinson to the odd looking man. She spoke in a friendly but slightly condescending way, 'How are you today? Have you spoken to the other officers? Have they been able to help?'

'I have, thank you Miss…..I mean…Sergeant,' he spoke with a lisp and spittle began to collect round his bottom lip as he continued to converse. 'I hope they can help, I really do. It's getting worse you know! Good day.'

His lisping words were spoken with an innocence normally reserved for children and he tapped his head as he gave his leave before wiping the saliva from his lip with a dirty sleeve.

'Good day Mr Light,' Sergeant Robinson said cheerily.

They watched him walk out of the station before the Sergeant turned to the man behind the desk.

'What's that, the seventh time in the last two weeks?! What wondrous tales have been happening at 16 Ashgate Place now, Mills?' Sergeant Robinson asked.

'A regular then?' enquired Andrews.

'Oh yes. Mr Light is exactly as named; a shard of light in our day,' Mills replied. 'I think that's actually the ninth time in the last two weeks.' Mills flicked through a note pad on his desk, 'Yep that's the ninth.'

'Come through,' Sergeant Robinson beckoned to Andrews.

They walked through a heavy-duty door to the other side of the Perspex screen where Mills was sat. He smiled at them as they entered. Other members of the station approached them along the corridor to greet the new recruit and his tour guide.

'I asked some of the team to meet us,' she said to PC Andrews in a friendly tone.

As Sergeant Robinson listed each person in turn they stepped forward to shake his hand. That was until she came to introduce Detective Norton. His brooding disinterest had been felt the moment Andrews had set eyes on him. PC Andrews had heard of Detective Norton's reputation. He had been quite the talk of the force with his arrest record and was held in high esteem. The talk of his successes where only matched by the rumours and tales of his unpredictable behaviour. He was said to be quite the charmer and a loyal friend though, once you proved yourself and got on the right side of him. The young constable knew this would take time and expected some kind of attitude from the outset. It was an honour that the detective had even showed up as part of the welcoming committee.

In an attempt to soften the hostility Andrews asked him as he extended his hand, 'I hear you have seen an interesting case this morning at the Areas building, downtown?'

Norton looked at the man's outreached hand but made no attempt to reciprocate the greeting. He looked in Andrews' eyes and made a low growl.

'Don't worry,' said Sergeant Robinson, gently taking PC Andrews' hand and lowering it down, 'Norton isn't the best conversationalist.'

'You met Mr Light then?' another PC said, bringing a sense of comedic relief to the meeting once more. 'What's he been saying this time?'

'Has the girl with impossibly long legs been following him again?' another chipped in and they all laughed. Even Norton's cheeks flexed at the humour.

Mills put his feet up on the desk in front of him and sighed, 'He believes he is being stalked and followed by an attractive women with long legs. Which obviously narrows it down a bit!'

'Well he did bring in that photo,' a PC added.

'That he did,' replied Mills, 'I've got it here. Not the most concrete evidence to go by.'

He handed to Andrews a blurry, pixilated photograph that must have been taken on a cheap mobile phone camera. Andrews studied it for a minute or two and began to make out a crowd of people in the city centre.

'Oh don't you see her?' said Mills. He wheeled his chair over, shuffling along with his feet whilst still remaining seated. He thumbed the photo, pointing at a space. 'Mr Light would have us believe that piece of wall was where the lady was when he took the photo. As soon as he took the photo she was gone.'

'So what happened today?' asked Andrews as he handed the photograph back.

'It appears this time Mr Light has seen the lady in question in his flat. He reports that she was looking

31

through his underwear drawer when he came in and disturbed her,' Mills explained in a deadpan manner.

The audience that had gathered round to hear the latest update burst into laughter and banter began to fly around the station.

'Ha ha, he'd be so lucky!' someone cried through their mirth.

'Disturbed her, he's the disturbed one,' screamed another.

'Bloody mentalist,' exclaimed PC Watts as he held his sides, 'he's the danger to her. A guy like that could probably kill a girl.'

Suddenly the laughing stopped and the mood tensed. Andrews was not sure what happened but reacted to the change as well. He looked at PC Watts cower and step backwards, away from the crowd.

'Oh Norton,' PC Watts said, his hands held up in a plea, 'I'm sorry.'

Norton grabbed Watts by the scruff of the neck and lifted him up with one of his big, oversized hands. He pulled the collar tight around the PC's neck. Watts began to splutter and choked out his words.

'I didn't mean it, I wasn't thinking,' Watts begged the big man to let him down.

Norton did not speak, but held his victim, studying him with a grimace. His eyes narrowed and his face screwed tighter with each passing moment. Everyone else stood back, unsure what was going to happen but knowing that something would.

'Norton!' a shout came from down the end of the corridor. 'Back down Norton and leave Watts alone!'

The stern, gruff voice was matched by an even sterner looking man marching down the corridor towards the crowd. His hands were tightly balled into fists and he wore a frown that had made many lasting creases across his face. His eyes gave the immediate look that he did not tolerate bullshit from anyone and those eyes were intently fixed on Norton and Watts.

Andrews sensed a stiffening in everybody's posture and the air seemed to thin as the man made his approach. Andrews made an educated guess that this must be Chief Inspector Hart.

Detective Norton was well known throughout the policing world as a great detective. He had an astounding arrest rate and the criminal world feared him, but handling him wasn't an easy job. That job was given to Chief Inspector Hart, or *No Heart,* as he was nicknamed (naturally behind his back). His was an even bigger legend and the stories of him single handedly taking out crime cartels had been talked of and passed down for so long, and by so many people, that it was impossible to pull the fact from fiction.

Andrews began to sweat uncontrollably with fear as Chief Inspector Hart approached. His presence held more authority and respect than any man Andrews had ever come across.

As the Chief Inspector marched ever closer Norton freed PC Watts from his chokehold and turned to face his superior.

Hart walked right up to him and, in front of everyone, let him have it.

'What do you think you are doing? This is no time to be fighting amongst ourselves! We have a mass homicide discovered in the Areas building, thirty dead, with no leads and no motive. The data is currently being processed in the lab but whilst that is going on I suggest you do what you do best; get out on the street, have a poke around and find out what you can. I suggest you detect, Detective!'

Hart stood still, nose to nose with Norton, without flinching or showing any intimidation despite the rotund subordinate being a good five to six stone bigger. Norton held his gaze in silent confrontation; eye to eye they were locked in a stand off, stretching each second into an event heavy with threat and anticipation. Then suddenly, without changing his expression Norton broke his intense stare, turned and walked out the station.

Everybody held their breath, unsure what to say or do. The only sounds were the rain against the window and the door swinging shut.

Hart turned and his eyes met Andrews' gaze. Once he had clocked the new recruit the stern features of confrontation melted into a pleasant and welcoming smile better suited to that of a first class airline cabin crew member than a gnarled Chief Inspector.

'PC Andrews I presume,' Hart took Andrews' hand and shook it gently but firmly, his other hand clutching at Andrews' elbow in a friendly gesture. 'Welcome to our police station, I'm sorry about Norton, he's one of the good guys really but he's had a tough time recently. You'll get up to speed soon enough and learn how we work, I've no doubt.'

He walked away, back to his office.

Everyone stood still and silent, frozen into

position until Hart was completely out of sight.

'Tough time?' Andrews asked, breaking the silence.

'Yeah,' Sergeant Robinson answered, her voice edged with sorrow, 'three weeks ago we get a call about some nut job that had run into a supermarket with a shotgun. Apparently he was going off his head screaming about how they were all after him. Real whacko. This guy grabs a hostage so back up is called for whilst the armed response arrive. Norton answers the call and arrives down there only to find the hostage is his girlfriend, Mel. Right in front of his eyes he watched this whacko off Mel point blank to the head with a shotgun, followed by himself. Real nasty like. Poor bastard, Norton couldn't even get his revenge.'

'Oh god,' Andrews responded sympathetically, 'should he be on duty?'

'He's a good cop. One of the best,' Sergeant Robinson explained. She glanced down the corridor making sure Chief Inspector Hart was in his office and out of earshot. 'Detective Norton is one of the few people I know that lives for his job, and right now it's all he has. CI Hart made the call to let him come back to work early. I guess he figured if he didn't Norton would probably kill himself.'

4

It's like killing yourself. A slow suicide.

Norton's thoughts were morbid whilst he swirled the last remaining mouthfuls of lager round the glass and contemplated the effects of alcohol on the liver.

He knew he shouldn't have lost his temper like he did back at the station; the Chief Inspector was right to have thrown him out. However he hadn't gone back to work but instead decided to seek comfort in a drink. He had made his way to the Black Ship Inn and found himself an isolated table to pick over his inner torments.

The pub was quiet with only three other patrons enjoying a drink. Enjoying a drink or escaping? They didn't look like they'd stopped off in their lunch break; in fact they didn't look like they'd been to work in a long while.

The carpet of the pub was mainly an off red, but with brown and yellow plant-like motifs weaving throughout. It was the kind of carpet seen in most pubs that hadn't been redecorated since the 1970s. Despite it only being a few hours into the afternoon the carpet was already grubby and clung to Norton's feet as he had moved from the bar to his seat. It probably wasn't due for its monthly clean for a while yet as he could still make out the plant-like pattern; an ingenious choice by the decorator so it could cleverly hide pools of vomit, and most probably did.

Norton had lost count of the time he'd been sat there and used the four empty pint glasses on his table as a marker to suggest it had been two hours. His mind kept rolling back to the same recent events that had troubled him for weeks and his face tightened like a screwed up piece of paper.

Why couldn't he have saved her?

Poor Mel.

Pretty Mel.

His mind cast back to those terrible events that blew his world apart and changed everything forever.

The supermarket had been sealed off. No one was getting in or out. It was him, Mel and the fucking loon.

He shouldn't have been in there, he should have been holding the perimeter and waiting for armed response. But the moment he saw Mel held helpless in her captor's arms he had no choice but enter the building. To try and reason with him.

Try and reason with him?!

Norton was not a reasonable man. He had never reasoned with anyone in his life. His fists made sure he got his own way most of the time when he was younger, and when he grew up his size and job made him more than intimidating enough to substitute fights. Mel was the only one that got one over on Norton, and she used to do that regularly. But size or authority mattered little to the man holding a shotgun to the head of his loved one whilst screaming inane, paranoid babble.

Norton had never been that close to losing something so precious, and when he was faced with it, when it mattered, he blew it.

At first, he remembered, he tried speaking to the man, asking him what he wanted. Edging closer and closer to the aggressor and hostage. But his words did not seem to sink in.

He tried again but the crazed man did not listen and just shouted back *I'll never be safe, you can't stop them, they're after me!* His rant did not let up. Nothing Norton said made any impact in stemming his delusions. Reason was beyond lost.

At that moment, realising nothing could be done, Norton had never felt so helpless. Tears of frustration had built up quietly behind his eyes and his breathing became laboured like there was an enormous pressure on his chest.

And then…

Then it all went into a blur.

He lost control.

Lost control and lost everything.

A matter of seconds is all it took to erase a life planned out between them.

His patience snapped as his frustration boiled over. Norton reached out to grab the man. If he could take his gun he could take away the threat. Then man-to-man he would take this lunatic down. But as he grabbed for the firearm the man stepped to the side and swung with the butt of his weapon. It was a lucky strike, but a strike none-the-less, and the contact to the side of Norton's head knocked him to the ground.

Still dazed, and with his cheek bleeding from the impact, he turned back to face them.

And then, as close as if he had pulled the trigger himself, he watched her die.

Her head seemed to explode into fragments like a glass vase hitting the ground from a great height. Her skull obliterated into red, fleshy pieces and her blood showered both of them.

Norton went numb, whether it was the deafening sound of the shotgun blast he could not say but everything seemed to stop. The stillness did not last and when the shotgun was pointed at him he found strength, picked himself up and ran for cover. Why was it then he found the strength? Only then he found the courage; the courage to run away.

Norton ducked into a shopping aisle, trying to use the shelving unit as shelter. As he ran for cover a shotgun blast grazed his shoulder. The wounded detective lay on the ground in pain, clutching his shoulder and trying to catch his breath. Another shot rang out followed by a horrifying *thud*. Trying to stay hidden he crawled on his front and peaked round the corner of the aisle. At first he saw nothing then he looked at the ground to see the man's body crumpled to the floor, a huge hole in his head oozing with blood. Both Mel and the lunatic lay dead; their corpses slumped together like faceless piles of lifeless flesh.

Norton stared out the window of the Black Ship Inn at the passing traffic as tears began to silently inch down the tough skin of his cheeks. He held his hand over his mouth so as to prevent any sound from escaping and felt himself getting angry that he was beginning to cry. Not here, not now, not Norton.

'Excuse me friend, do you mind if I take a seat here?'

Norton was momentarily taken away from his misery by a man in a grey suit. His dark hair was well groomed and recently cut; he placed a hand on the detective's shoulder as he sat down next to him.

'Hope you don't mind,' the man said, 'I'm Alex. I've just been for an interview and, lucky me, it finished just before the footy started. Are you a Wolves fan?'

Alex gave the grin of a salesman and had the confident patter to match.

'I'm sorry,' said Norton, turning his big frame towards this unwelcome companion, 'I want to be alone.'

'Oh,' the salesman said and looked around the pub, 'the thing is I really want to see this game and this is the only seat left to view the screen.'

Turning around himself Norton noted that the pub had indeed begun to fill whilst he had been lost in his internal meditations. Supporters from both sides had gathered, eager to watch the game.

'Unusual it's on today, I'll admit that,' said Alex, 'but you get a waterlogged pitch on the weekend then you have to take the re-plays when they come.'

Norton gripped his pint glass and squeezed,

trying to contain his anger, 'I just want to-'

'Should be a close game though,' Alex cut in, ignoring Norton, 'both are vying for top positions in the league and both with new managers, well, there's a lot to prove. I don't know if you've been following either side recently but both have produced outstanding football, just a shame about the weather. But then England wouldn't be England without a bit of rain. You can't have a green and pleasant land without any water to keep the land green and pleasant, you know what I mean? Crisp?'

He held his open packet to Norton offering him the contents but was immediately thrown off the chair by a punch from the disgruntled detective.

Alex rose to his feet from across the pub, where he had landed, and stroked his jaw.

'You got one hell of punch there,' he said, 'but that was uncalled for you mean old bastard. Anyone ever put you down before?'

'They've tried,' replied Norton.

Alex swung a right hook hitting Norton squarely on the cheek. The connection was good and took Norton off his feet. He fell backwards and landed on the table knocking the empty glasses to the floor with a dramatic crash. Norton was surprised by the power of the blow; the suit Alex wore hid a lot of strength.

Climbing off the table he got to his feet again but was greeted with a left, right to his stomach. Norton doubled up with the pain, and in doing so allowed Alex to take hold of his head. Alex pulled at his hair to get a better grip and Norton could see the intention was to ram him headfirst into the window. Reaching up and behind, Norton wildly grabbed, catching hold of Alex's shirt; he yanked suddenly, pulling Alex backward. Alex loosened his grip as he stumbled on his heels looking for balance. Norton continued his movement and grabbed the man's back with his other hand, picking Alex clean off the ground. With a huge effort Norton threw Alex against the bar, patrons dove out the way so as not to be hit by the human projectile as he crashed into the solid wood. Defeated, Alex groaned as he lay on the floor, his hand held up for the dual purpose of both protection and submission.

Norton relaxed from his fighting stance and saw the crowd stood around watching in disbelief.

'Sorry,' Norton said as he understood the spectacle he had just created.

'Fer Christ's sake Norton,' the barman complained, clearly annoyed as he began straightening up the furniture that had been knocked over during the fight, 'what the hell are you doing? You're a cop! Get out of here before I call one of your own.'

Yes I am a cop, thought Norton as he left the Black Ship, the rain washing him sober like a cold shower. What the hell was he doing getting into barroom brawls? This is not what Mel would have wanted. He was a cop, a bloody good one too, and she would not have wanted to see him end his days a brawling drunk. He nursed his cheek as he walked with purpose along the wet streets.

That punch got him good. Five years ago he was taking down punks like that without breaking a sweat. He was getting older and slower. It wouldn't be long before he was bested in a fight and if it got out of hand that could be the end of him. If you aren't in control a fight could very quickly escalate into death, accidental or not the outcome is still the same. Norton shuddered at the sights he had scene patrolling the brawl filled streets on a Saturday night.

The evening was beginning to draw in as Norton came to the Areas building. He was a cop all right and he had a purpose. Thirty dead: no witnesses, no motives, and no suspects. He looked up at the windows of the sixth floor to see the lights were on whilst he rubbed his throbbing head. He had a case to solve and a lot of coffee to drink.

It had only been ten hours ago that the building was crawling with police and every passage way blocked by crime scene tape. All that was gone when Norton entered the shiny marbled hallway of the Areas building foyer, sipping a recently purchased coffee from across the road. The only hint of the tragedy that had occurred was an LED light display over one of the lift doors flashing *Out Of Order*. He made his way to the sixth floor and was astonished to see a clean, brightly lit office. He checked the floor number on the wall to make sure he had got off on the correct floor, and was alarmed to see it did read as Floor 6. It was the same floor; the clean up operation had been fast.

He walked through the entrance of the office to see an irritated man with a wispy beard, thin wire glasses and wearing a faded Rammstein T-shirt.

'Who are you?' the bearded man asked with anger, his arms overloaded with keyboards, mice and other computer related pieces. Wires dangled dangerously from his load and threatened to trip him up.

'I'm Detective Norton,' replied Norton, showing him his credentials. 'Who the hell are you?'

'Ah you're a cop. I thought you'd have all finished with this place by now. I'm George; I'm the IT guy. Well I should be the IT guy, but I seem to have spent the last half of the day cleaning dried blood from between buttons of keyboards. Not in my job description!' he protested indignantly. 'Still it's good money.'

'People will do almost anything for money,' Norton dryly remarked. 'So you work here? But you weren't around when the incident happened?' he questioned.

'Good God no. I stay away from here as much as I can. Work from home mostly,' informed George. 'Most of the actual issues can all be resolved over the network. I have complete access to everything from home. It's only when I need to do any hardware changes I have to come in. That's usually once or twice a month if I can help it. I'm not much of a people person really.'

'You don't say?' said Norton, almost sympathetically. 'There's still a lot of investigation that needs to be done. If I can just take down your address and contact details, I may need to speak with you again.'

George sighed at the thought of being held up in leaving for the day, but knew it was useless to comment or fight and so gave his details to the detective.

'Can I go now?' barked George after Norton had the details he requested. 'I have had a very long and unusual day. I just want to get home.'

'Sure,' said Norton stepping aside to let him past.

George stomped by, heading to a storage cupboard to offload his armfuls before heading out into the night.

'You dropped something,' said Norton bending down to pick up the item.

George stopped and looked back, 'Oh that's just a flash drive, they are ten a penny round here. You can keep it.'

'No thanks,' replied Norton, 'I don't like the name on it.'

'Name?' George asked, taking the flash drive with his free hand. 'Oh. Ha. *Mel*. They're good quality these *Memory Inc* drives.' George slipped the flash drive into his left, front jeans pocket. 'So who is Mel?' he said as he opened the cupboard and casually threw his technological load in without caring to look where it landed. 'An ex?'

'Sort of,' Norton replied.

George packed up his equipment and prepared to head home whilst Norton sat down in one of the new chairs that had been shipped in that day to replace those soaked with blood and vomit from yesterday's atrocity.

What had happened here? He thought to himself. Someone turns all the cameras off then gases the place? But there was no sign of any contamination. And why this place? What has anyone got against a recruitment company? A disgruntled employee? Was that even what this company did? He made a mental note that he needed to check that.

Did George have anything to do with it? He had access to all the computer systems from a remote location. Could he have had access to the security systems? The lift controls? It was certainly worth further investigation.

Why did the lift crash? The mechanics report said there was no evidence of foul play; the only damage came from the impact. It was like the lift just hurtled down the shaft at break neck speed of its own accord.

Norton slumped forward resting his elbows on a desk and held his brow; despite the coffee he'd drunk he could still feel the effects of a hangover pulsating in his head. He sat back on the chair and began to feel tired. The comfort of his brand new seat began to relax his tense muscles. The fight had really taken it out of him earlier today.

He looked at the office in its new condition, shining and gleaming; a world away from the sight he beheld this morning. That was the modern world, he guessed. Tidy everything up and keep going. What was the saying? *Keep Calm and Carry On.*

Business has no time to grieve, he pondered, no soul to heal. Money must be made; work must continue.

His mind began to drift idly as his eyelids slowly closed and sleep took its hold.

J. R. Park

5

J. R. Park

His muscles felt limp and relaxed despite the confused and panicked state of his mind. It was dark and he was lost. He tried to move but his body refused to obey his commands. It was like Norton's whole body had gone to sleep but his mind had not followed.

Two figures began to grow visible from the dark surroundings. His heart stopped as he recognised the two ghosts before him. One with a crazed expression held a shotgun to the head of the other who looked terrified; her expression pleaded to Norton.

'Mel!' Norton gasped.

He tried to move again, hoping that this extra motivation would inspire life in his limbs, but the extra effort yielded the same results. He lay helpless as if he was a passenger, as if he was in someone else's body, as he watched the silhouetted lunatic aim the gun towards him.

Bang!

A shot fired and hit Norton in the shoulder.

His arm felt wet and hot as the top of his shoulder disintegrated in the blast, the pain coursed through his body.

More shots were fired, one after another, aimed directly at him as he lay motionless. Norton felt his stomach rip open and his intestines began to spill out onto his feet. Another shot shattered his left kneecap, the bone splintered into tiny pieces. His leg dangled, hanging on by a thread of flesh and skin. The third shot knocked him sideways as his hip exploded in a crimson shower. He tried to scream in pain but no sound came from his throat. He clenched his teeth together; the pain was unbearable and he prayed the next shot would kill him. He wished he would die.

'If I could get the gun from him,' Norton thought, 'I'd finish myself.'

He fell on to his front and felt a form of weak control return to his broken body. Clawing at the ground he slowly crawled forward toward the pair, with all the effort he could muster. Pulling what was left of himself along the floor he left a red, slippery trail behind him like some form of hellish slug.

Suddenly faces started to appear out of the gloom, screeching and babbling as they became visible. One by one they rushed towards Norton, howling in his face like they were mocking him. Blood oozed from the ragged stumps of their bitten off tongues. As each one howled they collapsed to the floor, dying; making horrific choking sounds and barely human screams as they perished. Pulling himself through the corpses of these tortured souls he finally reached the man with the shotgun and saw the corpse of Mel at his feet.

'Oh Mel,' he wept and hugged her lifeless body. Half her face had been shot away, 'Not again. I can't do it anymore.'

Suddenly he felt a tugging on his neck as the mad man grabbed the scruff of Norton's collar and picked him up with freakish strength, lifting him up until they were level, eye to eye. As he stared into those dark, wild eyes he could see no trace of compassion or understanding. He felt the cold barrel of the shotgun push against his chin.

'This must have been how Mel felt,' thought Norton.

As the gun went off Norton did not feel any impact of the shot. At first he felt his chin slowly crumble, both bone and skin breaking up into a fine powder. His nose followed suit and blood sprayed, as if in slow motion, as his nasal cavity tore to pieces. He watched his own teeth fly loose from his mouth and felt his tongue rip in half. The piece of tongue that remained had no jaw left to rest in so hung down loose by his neck, like a grotesque tie. The roof of his mouth cracked into fragments and as he felt his head split open he hoped this was the moment he had been waiting for. This was the moment he was going to die.

Darkness.

His muscles felt limp and relaxed, despite the confused and panicked state of his mind. It was dark and he was lost. He instinctively brought his hands to his face and despite the metallic taste of blood in his mouth he was relieved to feel his chiseled jaw was in one piece.

Norton looked around and realised he was still in the offices of the Areas building. How long had he been asleep?

It was dark and he remarked to himself how George must have turned the lights out on him. The windows let some light in from the street lamps outside to illuminate the edges of the room but did not penetrate any further, making it tricky to navigate around the desks and chairs. Norton moved slowly with his hands out so as to feel any obstacle in his path. Cautiously he made it to the edge of the room and began to feel around the wall looking for a light switch. There had to be one here, somewhere.

He groped the wall until his hand stumbled upon a small plastic box, he recognised the shape and hit the switches. The first few lights closest to him came on, the sudden brightness caused him to squint and he momentarily shielded his eyes whilst they adjusted.

At the far end of the office, still in semi darkness, he saw a woman dressed in a long, brown trench coat that went down to her knees. The woman had Japanese features and was startlingly attractive. Her shoulder length black hair flowed freely as she turned to face him. The coat was undone and revealed that she was wearing a black top and leggings with a pair of black leather boots that went all the way up to her toned thigh. Still groggy from his sleep Norton rubbed his eyes. Was he still dreaming?

The sharp kick to his ribs immediately answered that question.

In the space of a few seconds the woman had bolted across the room and hit him square in the chest with a well placed flying kick. He stumbled on his feet, disorientated. Another powerful kick hit Norton on the jaw, sending him crashing against a wall and then to the ground.

Shaking it off, he got to his feet and gave chase as his assailant sped away. She had misjudged her route and missed the doorway, her exit now looked blocked as they came to a wall, a dead end. He held his arms out to grab his trapped target, but without breaking stride she jumped into the air and did a back flip over him. With honed reactions he reached up with his big hands and caught an ankle, slamming her down to the ground with a hard thump. The woman hit her head hard on the ground as she landed; her eyes rolled behind her eyelids and she lay still, groggy and stunned.

'Who the hell-?' Norton's question was interrupted and attention diverted as, without warning, all the lights in the office blazed on, bathing the fighters and their surroundings in harsh, electric light.

A voice boomed across the room as men in suits marched in, the man in the middle, obviously the leader, making all the noise.

'What the hell? It's been cleaned already?'

The man wore a pin striped suit. It fitted too well against his frame to be an off the peg purchase. He was average looking in build, but Norton had already been fooled by how a suit could conceal muscle once today. The man had jet black hair, was clean shaven and well groomed. The other men followed him, slightly behind and listened intently to his every word.

'I can't believe it's been cleaned already. They had better have used the scanner. I want this building sealed off. No one in. What the hell is he doing here?'

Remembering his fight Norton looked back to find an empty space where a beautiful and very aggressive Japanese woman had laid. Angry with himself for letting her get away he chose not to mention anything to these people. He could never trust a man whose suit cost more than his own monthly mortgage repayments.

'Who the hell are you?' asked Norton.

'Who the hell am I!' the man replied, his aggressive tone had not abated since his startling entrance. 'Who the hell are you?'

'Detective Norton,' he answered obligingly. 'I'm investigating the deaths that happened here.'

'We're investigating the deaths that happened here,' the man in the expensive suit barked. 'I'm Royal. MI5. This is our case now. I want you out of the building in fifteen minutes.'

Two of Royal's men approached Norton from either side to usher him out.

'So this is what a cop looks like now-a-days huh?' scoffed Royal. 'Can somebody search him please?'

The two men searched through his pockets. Norton held his hands up and let them carry on. He had been in enough scrapes already today, this battle with MI5 could wait, he was sure he would see them again.

On searching Norton the two men found a wallet, a phone, his warrant card, standard issue handcuffs, a small bottle of whiskey (half empty), a receipt for a takeout coffee and a carefully folded piece of paper with a hand written message on it.

It read:

> *Back soon.*
> *Love you.*
> *Mel xxx.*

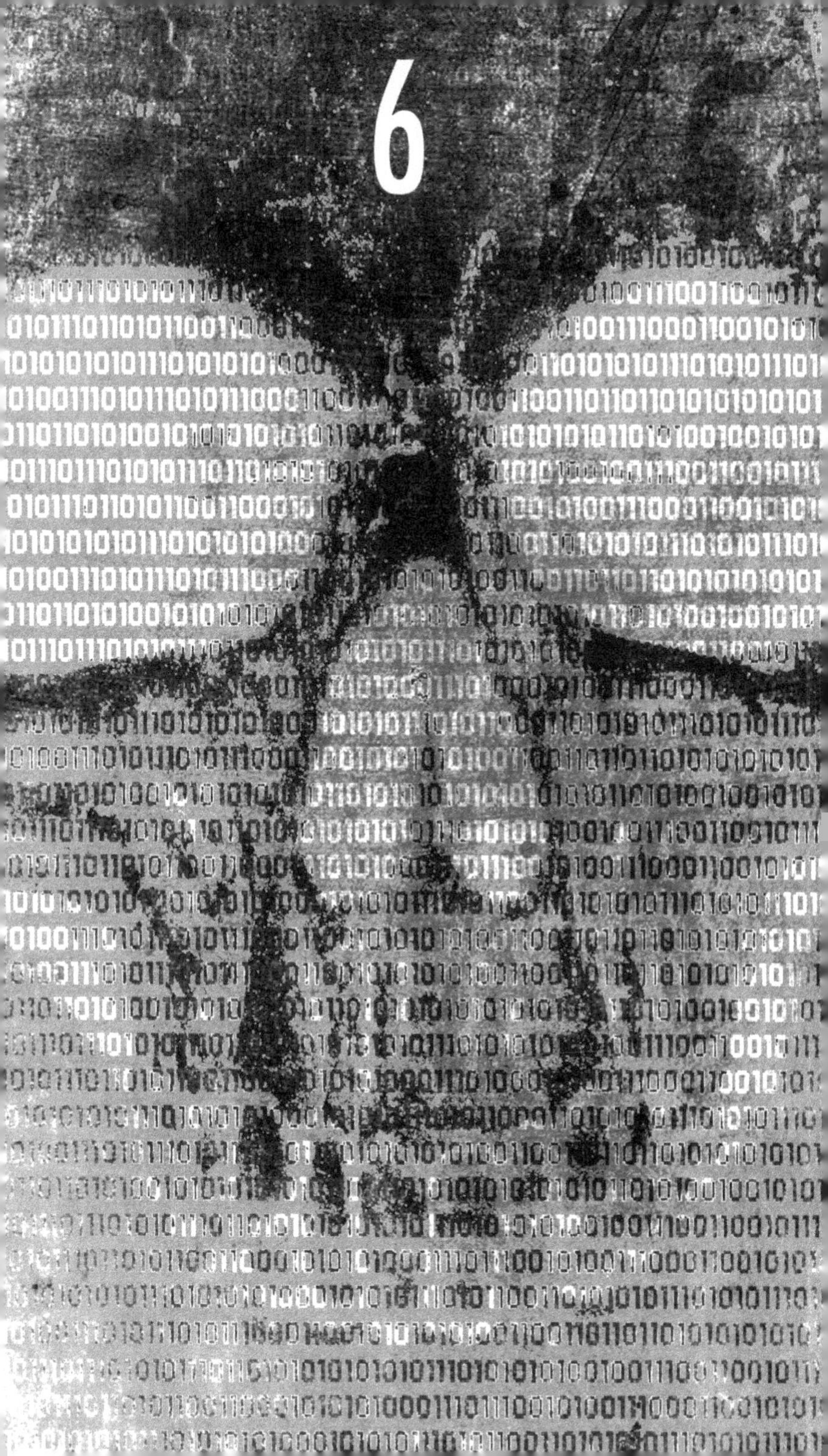
6

'You're off the case,' Chief Inspector Hart often looked stern, but this was a level of anger that was rare in him. His hardened features started to turn red as blood filled his cheeks and his temper began to boil over.

In rage he had stood to his feet, knocking his chair over and slamming his fists into the papers that covered the work surface of his crowded desk. He stared directly into Norton's equally seething eyes. It was due to times like this that his office had been sound proofed decades ago.

After his run in with the MI5 yesterday Norton had headed home to sleep off the hangover and bruises that had marked a turbulent day. He was in the station early the next morning and made his way directly to CI Hart's office to discuss the MI5 intervention. It seemed Hart had been in for hours and was expecting Norton's rant. He seemed fully aware of the situation and didn't seem happy either, especially to be caught in the middle.

'Not only are you off the case', Hart continued

to put Norton in his place, pointing his figure in short, aggressive motions, 'there is no case. MI5 came in yesterday. They took the case over then closed it down.'

'They did what?' Norton was about to escalate the verbal assault that had been cut off before its prime. Sadly he was denied again as Hart jumped back in.

'Oh like you I was curious,' Hart shouted, 'so I tried to find out what was going on. I have been on the phone for hours and tried everyone I know. You know the most I got? *MI5 have the matter in hand.* That's it.'

'You can't just let them do that,' protested Norton.

'Do you know how hushed up this is? I spoke to people in the agency that owes me their lives and all I get back is the same *MI5 have the matter in hand.* I met a wall of silence, the likes of which I have never encountered before. This is big and goes to the top.' Hart's honesty was a clear symptom of the frustration he was having with this affair, 'It's best we keep clear and let them do their business, Detective. They are coming in today to remove the last pieces of evidence we have here. You may want to make yourself scarce!'

'I'll be here,' Norton had calmed down slightly, realising that Hart was not the enemy here and could do nothing further. 'I have a job to do.'

Norton left the Chief Inspector's office and headed deeper into the station. His mind was racing with questions. What had happened? Why had MI5 got involved and more importantly why had they closed the case down? He needed answers. It was against everything he stood for to leave those deaths unsolved.

What if it happened again? He couldn't let that rest on his conscience. He had already let one person die, it wouldn't happen again.

He still had very little in the way of leads to go on, but the latest mystery to be added to the case was the appearance, and subsequent disappearance, of the beautiful Japanese woman. Beautiful but deadly he reminded himself as he rubbed his bruised side. Why was she there and what was she doing? Who was she and how did she connect with the deaths?

Norton made his way to a small room where a uniformed policeman was sat in front of a computer terminal.

'Greeves,' Norton greeted the man with a nod.

'Hey Norton, how are you today?' Greeves looked up from his computer screen and gave a smile. 'What can I do you for?'

'I need you to run a photo fit for me. See if we have any information on a potential suspect I ran into last night,' Norton asked whilst taking a seat next to his colleague. The detective's large frame dwarfed the chair as he sat down.

The two chatted for half an hour as first Norton explained what had happened last night then described the woman's features, bit by bit. Greeves listened and selected features on the computer following the description. He asked further questions and made refinements to the profile, widening and narrowing spaces between features until Norton was satisfied with the outcome. The detective had done this many times before so he knew the procedure and he knew to not stop until it was as best as his memory would allow.

'That's it,' said Norton with achievement in his voice when they had finally completed the photo fit.

'She's certainly pretty. Let's have a look and see what we have,' said Greeves as he began to run the image through the database, checking for any matches.

The program took a few minutes to complete its checks and the two waited with anticipation.

'Bingo,' exclaimed Greeves, 'you are good Norton, we've got a perfect match.'

The two leaned closer to the computer as information appeared on the screen.

Greeves read it out aloud, 'Only known as Orchid, real name: unknown. Family: unknown. Birthplace: unknown. Current location: unknown. It seems we have a right little mystery on our hands.' He turned to Norton, 'Let's look at the intel.' He turned back to the screen and scrolled through different tabs of information, 'Here we go, your mystery girl is a known mercenary. There are warrants out for her arrest in connection to murders seemingly in the sphere of the rich and influential. Well, well, she was behind the death of that German diplomat a couple years back. Looks like it wasn't really a heart attack. Mostly though it seems she is a thief. Operates around the world with photos and reports of her in many different countries.'

'A high flyer,' Norton commented.

'Indeed. Slippery too,' Greeves added, his tone suggested he was impressed with what he read, 'looks like she has only been caught once. Detained by authorities in Brazil five years ago. She escaped, but not before a slaughter of half the station.'

'She doesn't like to be cornered, I can vouch for

that,' Norton leaned back in his chair. It groaned under his weight.

'She normally packs a Samurai sword under that big coat of hers. Norton you got off lightly,' he half joked.

'Not you guys too!' Sergeant Robinson said as she walked past and put her head round the door.

'What?' asked Norton.

'You're looking at the new hottie too! She was transferred over today. The boys have been lusting over her all morning. You can practically cut the air it's so thick with hormones.'

'New transfer?' quizzed Norton. 'Her?'

He pointed to the picture on the computer screen.

'Yeah. That's PC Pearce,' she took the mouse and changed the view to the security cameras of the station, flicking between them before stopping on one view. 'There she is, down in evidence.'

Norton and Greeves leaned closer and compared the image on the camera view to that from the photo fit database. She was wearing a police uniform, but there was no mistaking those alluring features. It was Orchid.

The station had never felt so vast as Norton bolted out of the photo fit lab and ran down to the lower level where the evidence room was located. He had to admit that Orchid was bold to walk into a police station undercover, but her confidence would be her undoing.

He almost fell down the stairs, making an ungainly entrance into the evidence room as he slipped and tumbled. The sudden crash of Norton coming through the door startled Orchid who turned around to see who had disturbed her.

'You may be dressed like one but you're no cop. I know who you are, Orchid,' Norton gasped as he caught his breath. 'I've got you trapped. You've nowhere to go.'

Orchid looked at the wheezing detective and gave a wry smile, 'You had me cornered before. It didn't work out well for you then did it?'

'It's just me and you this time,' Norton said as he walked towards her.

Orchid used the pile of weapons amassed as evidence to her advantage. Picking up a knife she threw it at Norton, aiming it at his head. He dived to the floor, dodging the blade as it buried itself into the wall behind him. Using the distraction Orchid picked up a crude, homemade mace constructed of nails driven into a baseball bat, and swung it, smashing a window next to her. The window led out onto a ramp from the underground car park and to freedom. With speed and agility she vaulted through the make shift exit so when Norton got back to his feet he was confronted with an empty room.

A broken window signified to him where his attacker had fled.

Norton's ungraceful attempt at crawling through the window was the exact opposite of the fleeting dive Orchid had succeeded in. Halfway through he questioned why he didn't just go back out through the main entrance, but he was committed now. He pulled

his large frame through and made it outside, just in time
to see Orchid duck into an unused factory that
neighboured the station.

He ran in after her but stopped his pursuit to let his eyes
adjust to the darkness. The building had not been used
for at least half a decade. The windows were caked with
a brown filth, a collection over the years of all the dirt
and fumes the active estates pumped into the air. Light
struggled to penetrate the grime leaving the inside
bathed in a dim, brownish glow. When his eyes grew
accustomed to the low level of light he saw that the
place looked deserted; had he not seen Orchid enter
with his own eyes he would have given up the search,
there was no sign of her anywhere. He moved quietly,
not wanting to make a sound and strained his eyes to see
through the gloom.

He felt a blow to his shoulder, knocking him
forward. Leaving her hiding place in the rafters Orchid's
foot had connected with his back as she landed on the
detective. Her thighs gripped his neck and her legs
locked around him. The force of her surprise attack
knocked Norton to the floor and he landed hard onto
his front. Orchid jumped off her human target landing
with grace and control behind him. With a heavy boot
she spread his legs and kicked hard between them.
Using his thighs as a guide she hit directly centre, landing
the end of her boot squarely on his groin.

Norton let out a groan of pain and all the air
escaped from his lungs.

'You men are so weak,' she taunted as she
circled him, 'so easy to hurt.'

He reached out and caught her ankle, pulling her legs from under her; she toppled and landed on her back.

'You're not so invincible yourself,' he quipped back.

Norton got to his feet and made his way to where Orchid lay on the dusty ground. As he approached her she rolled backwards, then using her arms to launch herself, she flipped forward and flew through the air. One foot connected with his face, the other hit his stomach. He fell backwards in pain, but before he had time to hit the floor Orchid gave him a powerful upper cut to the jaw, followed quickly by sweeping his legs from under him with a swift movement from her well-toned thigh.

Battered and disorientated Norton stumbled back to his feet but the blows from Orchid rained down thick and fast. He fell against a wall and held his hands out to steady himself, in doing so his fingers found a piece of loose wood. Grabbing the newly found weapon he swung at Orchid who ducked and avoided the blow. He swung again trying to catch her, but this time she carefully stepped to the side and countered by punching him in the back of the head. He stumbled forward and tripped.

'You keep coming back for more don't you?' Orchid taunted him again.

He turned around to face her and only had time to get to his knees before her boot cracked against the side of his head. Another boot came towards him, but this time he was ready and held up the piece of wood he had in his hand. The wood broke in two with the power of the kick but the unexpected connection caught Orchid off balance. Using the break between the blows Norton took one half of the wood and slugged it hard against the side of her head. The blow connected squarely and its strength knocked Orchid to the floor. She lost consciousness before she hit the ground.

Orchid awoke still in the abandoned factory. She found herself slumped forward, sat on a chair with blood running down her cheek. Her hands were cuffed behind her back and rope tied round her waist, securing her to the chair. Norton did not want to take any chances. She tried to struggle but felt the cuffs tighten as she did, causing pain to shoot up her wrists.

'You're awake then?' the voice was Norton's.

She looked up to see him stood in front of her, pacing from left to right and back again.

'I don't know what's going on,' Norton continued without letting her answer, 'but I'm not going to take you back to the station until I have some answers. MI5 are all over this and as soon as they have you I doubt I will ever see you again. What is your involvement in the deaths at the Areas building? Who has hired you and why?'

'Don't be a fool,' she scoffed, 'you don't have a clue.'

'I found this in your pocket,' he held up a creased photo with fold marks down the middle. Its condition suggested it had been handled a lot. 'What do you want with this?'

The photo showed the picture of a flash drive. It was battered and damaged and half its writing had been worn away. What was left seemed to make up a word.

Mel.

7

J. R. Park

George's fingers had begun to turn puffy and wrinkly like out of date cocktail sausages due to the amount of time he had been in the bath. He checked his fingers over one last time. After the twenty minutes or so he'd spent scrubbing them he was pretty sure he'd got rid of all the blood. This was the fifth bath he had taken since coming home last night. He couldn't see any more on his hands and was well aware he was probably being a bit obsessive about the whole thing. He chuckled as he pictured himself like a modern day Macbeth, but it was disgusting having to clean all that equipment from the splatters of blood that had been in various different states of solidification.

He thought back to the office in the Areas building as he stepped out of the bath and dried himself. He didn't know them very well, but still, it was weird to think they were all gone. All dead. All at once.

Once dressed George opened the door from his bathroom to see the steam from the bath water had drifted into the rest of his small flat. His dwelling was small and compact, but it was just right for him. He kept it clean, particularly his cabinet in which sat his favourite models of science fiction characters. It stood tall in his living room, commanding attention, and was his pride and glory in his own little kingdom.

It was strange to think he was straight back to work after the deaths. He had been called in to the office again tomorrow. He didn't want to go but he had no choice. To the company it was about getting back to business as usual. All hands were on deck to help out with the recruitment of new staff. Overtime was offered to get it moving quicker, flat rate you understand. It always was!

George thought it a little distasteful and perhaps a few days should have been left to mourn and acknowledge the dead. But everyone else had voted to press on, the overtime was offered and they all could do with the money. It's amazing what people will do for money, he mused.

He picked up a sandwich that was half eaten by his computer and began to munch on it. What would be tonight's entertainment he thought as he turned his computer on and sat down in front of it. What was on tonight's porn stream? Last night he'd watched two girls fuck each other with a cucumber. That had certainly taken the edge off the day; a dirty smile grew from the corner of his mouth as he thought back to it. Now that was worth the money.

He noticed the flash drive he had found in the office during the tidy. That was a nice bit of equipment; a bit battered on the outside but if it worked then that's all that mattered. He inserted it into his computer to check his find was functional.

Norton had gotten little information from Orchid. She remained tied to the chair but Norton had decided violence would not be the way to get her to talk. It was only when he mentioned knowing the whereabouts of the sought after piece of hardware that she became forthcoming. Perhaps she thought if she gave him information she might get some in return. It didn't matter what he told her, she was incapacitated and would be going straight to a holding cell shortly.

'Contained on that flash drive,' she began, 'is an extremely sophisticated and extremely dangerous weapon. It's nicknamed the Death's Head program. It's a computer program created by the UK government; they've been using it for years. You can think of it as an electronic assassin if you will, and it's been the envy of all other governments and weapons developers. It was spoken about in hushed voices like a myth, something akin to a boogeyman, except it got the rich and powerful scared. Really scared. My employer was doing a deal to get a copy; someone had managed to download a copy on the flash drive in that photo. But something went wrong. It was lost.'

George was pleased to see the flash drive was working and held even more storage space than he had hoped. The connections were top of the range too which meant he had a fast and neat piece of kit. There had been a file on the memory stick so George had run a virus checker to make sure it was safe. The results came back fine.

The file was huge in size and simply titled *Execute*. Intrigued at what the program might be George double clicked the icon with his mouse.

Norton sat down in front of Orchid, absorbing the information she was giving but finding it hard to believe.

'It's a weapon,' she continued, 'it's used to infiltrate enemy computer systems and use those systems against them. I don't know why the office got hit yesterday but I'm assuming that someone had the flash drive and ran the program. The fact you've seen the stick confirms that for me. You have to tell me where it is. If for no other reason than to get it off the streets.'

'So what happened in the Areas building?' asked Norton, still not connecting everything together.

'Obviously the office that got hit yesterday didn't have any weapons so it must have improvised.'

'Improvised? How do you mean?' Norton rubbed his stubble, a pleasing feeling to comfort him whilst he heard the disturbing tale Orchid told.

'I've seen this before,' she said, her focus leaving the room for a moment whilst her thoughts turned inward to a memory, 'my employer was hit by it. That's how they found out about its existence. It can use the computer itself as a weapon.'

Setting target flashed up on George's screen. He couldn't work out what the program was doing and so far had been unimpressed by the user interface. The screen flickered; the computer's camera turned on and filled the display with George looking back at himself from the monitor. Startled at first, but then realising what had happened, he intently looked at his own image wondering what would happen next. The image began to change slightly, almost decay, and he noticed that bits of the graphic display began to fall away as if his face was melting. Piece after piece seemed to dissolve from the picture and roll down the screen, revealing the white of a skull underneath. Momentarily fearing the image was real he rubbed his hands across his face and was relieved to feel it all there. His heart pounded against his chest as he remained transfixed with this computer trick. As the image of his face continued to melt away George noticed the rest of the screen started to flash brightly and intensely, picking up speed until it flashed with the rhythmic pace of a strobe.

'I've heard reports of many tricks,' Orchid divulged. 'It will display something strange on the screen to get the targets interest and keep them fixed on it. Using strobes and images it can get people into a trance like state, almost hypnotized to the screen. It can continue with these strobe flashes to do a lot of damage. They can cause seizures, making people fit, foam at the mouth, bite off their own tongue.'

George felt rooted to his chair as his gaze remained firmly on the screen. He began to shake, his jaw locking at an angle and saliva building in his mouth to produce a foam that begin to spurt out between gritted teeth. He could hardly think straight but had to get away. He leaned back and tried to fall off his chair to break the gaze of the screen but he found it an impossible task. The image on the screen continued to melt, chunks of cheek and nose seemed to liquefy into a putrid mess and roll down the desktop until all that was left was a white, bloodied skull. The picture began to lose clarity when suddenly the skull changed from solid white to black and white static. Its edges shook and blurred, changing the shape of the skull and denying it any definition. The hideous graphic opened its skeletal jaw and roared through the speakers, as it did so an even more intense flash flared across the screen so bright that it would be the last thing George ever saw.

'Using the screen,' Orchid warned, 'it can create a flash bright enough to blind you. But it doesn't just rely on visual stimulus to make the computer a weapon. It can make the machine produce high-pitched sounds. The sonics can be at such a level that they can cause dizziness, disorientation and induce vomiting. They showed me footage of people that vomited until they couldn't breathe. Others went way beyond that, rupturing eardrums and bursting blood vessels in their brains. Slow, agonizing, messy deaths.'

George staggered around the flat in darkness. The flash had blinded him completely. He needed to find a phone, to find the way out and get help. A high-pitched noise began to come from the speakers of his computer. He held one hand over an ear and screamed with pain, the other hand he forced to keep out in front of him, searching for a wall. He fell into something tall and large. It came crashing down, hitting George and taking him with it. As the glass door smashed into shards he realised he'd knocked over his beloved model cabinet.

Getting to his knees the sound began to buzz in his head and a tightening gripped his stomach. Vomit was expelled violently up his throat and out through both his mouth and nose; the stinging taste of bile clung to his taste buds and he was sick again. He felt himself become light headed. Desperate for air he tried to breathe but the vomiting fits were relentless and he was unable to catch his breath in between his innard expulsions. It was only when his stomach had expelled its entire contents and half its lining that George could breathe again but by now it was too late. The high-pitched sounds had done their damage and caused blood vessels to rupture in his brain. He slumped forward, his hand just catching the door handle as his twitching, lifeless body hit the deck. Blood trickled from his ear and formed a crimson pool on the floor.

The high-pitched noises stopped, the screen reverted back to its normal desktop setting and everything was calm and still.

Norton was still quizzing Orchid about the Death's Head program and her story.

'The reason you have no evidence,' said Orchid, becoming somewhat impatient, 'is that it can get into the main frame of any system. It can wipe the cameras.'

She saw a hint of understanding in Norton's face; he had started to believe her.

'As I said,' she carried on, 'the Death's Head program was thought to be a myth, but one that people were still afraid of. No one knew exactly what it was and how it was doing what it was doing. My employer tried a number of tricks with isolated camera circuits, going back a bit in technology. They succeeded and managed to get some footage. The poor bastards,' her thoughts drifted sympathetically to those she had seen killed by its destructive power. 'Once it has completed its job it wipes itself from the computer, as if it never existed. Slick, sleek and deadly.'

'And who wants it?' Norton asked.

'I don't know who my employer is, rarely ever do,' answered Orchid. 'Just a guy with some interesting film footage, a photo of a flash drive and a whole lot of money.'

8

J. R. Park

Norton pulled up on the side of the street in his car and checked the numbers on the doors of the houses. He matched the number 18 with the address he'd taken from George. Number 18 flat 4. The street was made of large townhouses that had been bought up by landlords and divided into flats, then rented out to professional couples or students with wealthy parents. It attracted a bohemian element, apparent in the tasteful graffiti of spaceships and unicorns that adorned some of the houses. He rang on the buzzer and waited for an answer.

Looking down the quiet street he thought back to the stories Orchid had told him about the Death's Head computer program. Was it for real? It was certainly an explanation that made all the pieces fit together.

Once she'd spilled the story to him he'd taken her back to the police station and put her in a cell. She could be dealt with later. But what a criminal to have caught!

Whilst taking her back to the station he noted that MI5 had still not arrived, but was told they were on their way. This lead needed to be checked before they got their hands on it.

He pressed the buzzer again but still no answer. Thankfully a neighbour living in the same block came out of the front door to leave and let him in as they did so.

Norton made his way up the staircase to flat 4. He knocked on the door but as he expected no answer came. Using his large mass he smashed the door open by crashing his thick, heavy shoulder against the panel until it buckled under the force, knocking the weak screws from their hinges. These houses were poorly maintained by greedy landlords, they wanted the money but didn't want to spend anything on the upkeep and repair. Anything replaced in these places were of questionable craftsmanship. The doors included.

The smell of bile and urine hit him the instant he crashed through the door, his nose being immediately assaulted. The smell reminded him of the Areas building a few days ago and he feared the worst. Those fears were confirmed when he found the body of George lying face down on the floor surrounded in pools of his own vomit and blood. Not the most dignified way to go, Norton thought. Furniture had seemingly been thrown around the flat; the sitting room was trashed, but no sign of anyone else. Norton looked at the idle computer and saw the flash drive still inserted into the USB port, the scuffed markings on the battered casing read *Mel*. His heart quickened as he caught sight of the name. Reaching over he pulled it out and put it in his coat pocket for safekeeping. His timing couldn't have been better, for as soon as he had safely stowed the flash drive away he heard a voice he recognised from behind him.

'Detective Norton, what are you doing here? We must stop meeting like this!' It was Royal, the agent from MI5.

He entered the room and looked down at the body, a small grimace of disgust gripped his features.

'Oh dear,' Royal said, 'what a mess.'

'You knew about this!' Norton shouted at Royal. 'This whole mess is down to a piece of Government property.'

'Have you been talking to Orchid?' asked Royal. 'From the state of your bruised face it certainly looks like you two have been playing. I was informed you had her in a holding cell, and she informed us where to find you.'

'You can't cover this up Royal,' Norton protested, 'people need to know.'

'Do they?' asked Royal rhetorically. 'I don't think they do. There are a lot of things that people don't need to know.'

He stepped over George's body and picked up a chair from the floor. Righting it he took a seat, crossing his right foot over his left thigh, and relaxed into the back rest until it creaked.

'Why don't I tell you a little story about Jake?' Royal began. 'Jake gets up in the morning; he puts his clothes on in a rush and makes his way to his boring office job. On his way there he complains to himself about how boring his life is and he gets angry that the supermarket has run out of chocolate brioche again. Every morning he stops by to purchase chocolate brioche and every few days they have run out before he gets there. He is annoyed and continues his walk to work wondering why the supermarket can't get its ordering right to meet demand and where is he going to get his sweet fix from that morning. These things concern Jake, but these concerns are a luxury; a luxury brought about by living in a safe and protected country.' Royal's voice was eerily calm and collected as he spoke, 'We do a lot of things to afford Jake the ability to have a boring life, to have the luxury of getting angry about the stock levels of chocolate brioche in the mornings. And a lot of those things Jake doesn't need to know.' Royal remained seated, but narrowed his eyes and stared directly into Norton's, 'Give me that flash drive, Norton.'

'Not a chance,' came his reply.

Royal stood up and the two squared off to each other.

'Then I'll take it by force,' threatened Royal.

'We'll see about that,' challenged Norton.

Royal came at him with the skill and speed of a trained service man. A roundhouse kick to Norton's side proved he had good fighting technique and power to match. The kick connected heavily and Norton winced in pain. The bruised detective had been in a lot of fights over the last few days and he began to feel the tenderness of his injuries as Royal followed his kick with a powerful fist and punched him on his already damaged cheek. He stumbled to his knees and the pain reminded Norton he was getting too old for these kind of confrontations. Deep inside he just wanted to stay down. He knew getting up to fight would result in more punches and kicks being received but he knew he had to. Seeing another fist coming towards him Norton held his arm up and blocked the blow. Another tried to connect but again the detective deflected the attack, making Royal hit the wall. The MI5 agent's pain was clearly visible as his knuckles buried into the plaster. Norton took this cue to hit Royal hard on the cheek. The retaliation felt good as Royal fell to the floor, hitting his head and losing consciousness.

Norton checked Royal was still breathing then put the unconscious man's hands behind his back, locking his wrists together with a pair of handcuffs.

That should hold him for a while when he wakes up.

A quick search of the agent's pockets uncovered a set of car keys which Norton took with him.

He was glad of taking the keys. As he suspected he went back to his car to discover the tyres had been slashed, no doubt by Royal to make sure he couldn't get anywhere easily. Norton took the keys he had stolen and pressed the unlock button. Across the street a black BMW 5 series made a beeping noise and its lights flashed.

Bingo!

He ran across the road and jumped in the car. The key fitted perfectly into the ignition and started first time. The car roared as, excitedly, he revved the engine and drove off.

With the Death's Head program in his pocket he knew

he had the prize, but now what to do with it? Where to go? The city glided past the tinted windows as he made his way across its busy centre. His mind began to wander, thinking about his next course of action, so much so that he completely missed a set of traffic lights that were changing in front of him. He zipped through as they turned red, narrowly avoiding a car coming alongside his left on the crossroads. The other car honked its horn as it swerved wildly to miss him. Behind him Norton heard more horns beep and looked back to see two more black BMWs dodge the traffic to make the same dangerous journey he had just done.

They couldn't have just done the same as him? They would have been further away from the lights with plenty of time to stop. And they are both the same make of car!

Suspicions flew through his mind that he was being followed. The confirmation came when a shot was fired from one of the cars, hitting the side of Norton's vehicle.

Royal hadn't been alone.

As the chase began Norton knew he had the advantage. He'd worked in this city all his life and knew every road, every nook and cranny. Turning sharply he sped down a small alleyway with only inches to spare either side of the car. The other two followed him, but with the walls being so close they had no room to aim their guns out of the window. The cars bounced off the walls as they sped down the narrow alleyway, accompanied by a sound of scraping metal. Despite the minor bodywork damage they all made it through and emerged in the middle of St Paul's market. Glancing at his watch Norton knew the market would be packing up at this time. The crowds would be sparse but there would still be empty stalls, crates and vans in the middle of the road as the traders prepared to end their day of business and head home. Norton dodged between the obstacles but did not brake or slow up. The cars followed but the second car turned too late round some crates. The car arced out in a larger turning circle and smashed into the side of a parked van.

Norton caught the crash in his rear view mirror and couldn't help but raise a smile. That car wasn't going anywhere. One down, one to go.

They cleared the market and joined up with the motorway that ran through the city. He didn't want to put lives at danger but he had to shake his pursuer. He weaved in and out of lanes, past lorries and hoped that he could get enough traffic between himself and the MI5 agent that he might hide in the busy flow. This was not to be as the chasing agent stuck to him like glue. Every time Norton boldly cut lanes through a gap between an HGV and another vehicle the MI5 agent would do the same. In fact he was so intent on following Norton he was close to running people off the road.

Fearing more innocent people would be hurt Norton took a blocked exit onto the building site of a new road. It was late and most of the workers would have gone home by now. There would certainly be fewer cars to worry about. He crashed through the *No Entry* sign and sped forward. This new road was part of a bridge construction. It hadn't been completed or connected yet and Norton knew he was driving toward a man-made cliff face. Further along the road ascended as it went over the river, but it stopped halfway; the connecting piece was separated by a gap of 50 metres. He looked back to see the other car still hot on his tail as they sped past signs warning them of the bridges unfinished nature and the danger that lay ahead.

Could he make the jump? He wondered to himself as he held the accelerator firmly to the floor with his foot. The speedometer continued to increase 90 – 100 –110 – 120 mph. His pursuer had seen the bridge was out and understood what Norton's escape plan was. Like his target he too had his foot clamped to the accelerator and managed to catch Norton up. The two now drove side by side like they were competing in a drag race. The huge drop in the road grew closer and closer and as it did the gap seemed to grow wider and wider. It was going to take all their speed to make that jump.

Suddenly Norton turned the wheel hard and slammed on the brakes. His car turned 180 degrees and skidded to a stop; his back wheels inches from the edge.

He looked through the rearview mirror to see the MI5 agent drive off the road and plummet into the river below.

There was no way anybody could make that jump, he thought to himself. Damn fool had watched too many James Bond movies.

Norton caught his breath as he sat in the motionless car and tried to figure out what to do next when he heard a familiar voice from the back seat.

'Hello stranger. That was a wild ride.'

The silky tones of that voice were last heard confessing all she knew whilst tied to a chair in an abandoned factory. It was Orchid. Her hands were held behind her back where Royal had cuffed her for transportation. She had been laid down on the back seat all this time!

Orchid sat upright and smiled at his reflection in the rearview mirror.

'I hope you have what I'm looking for,' she said.

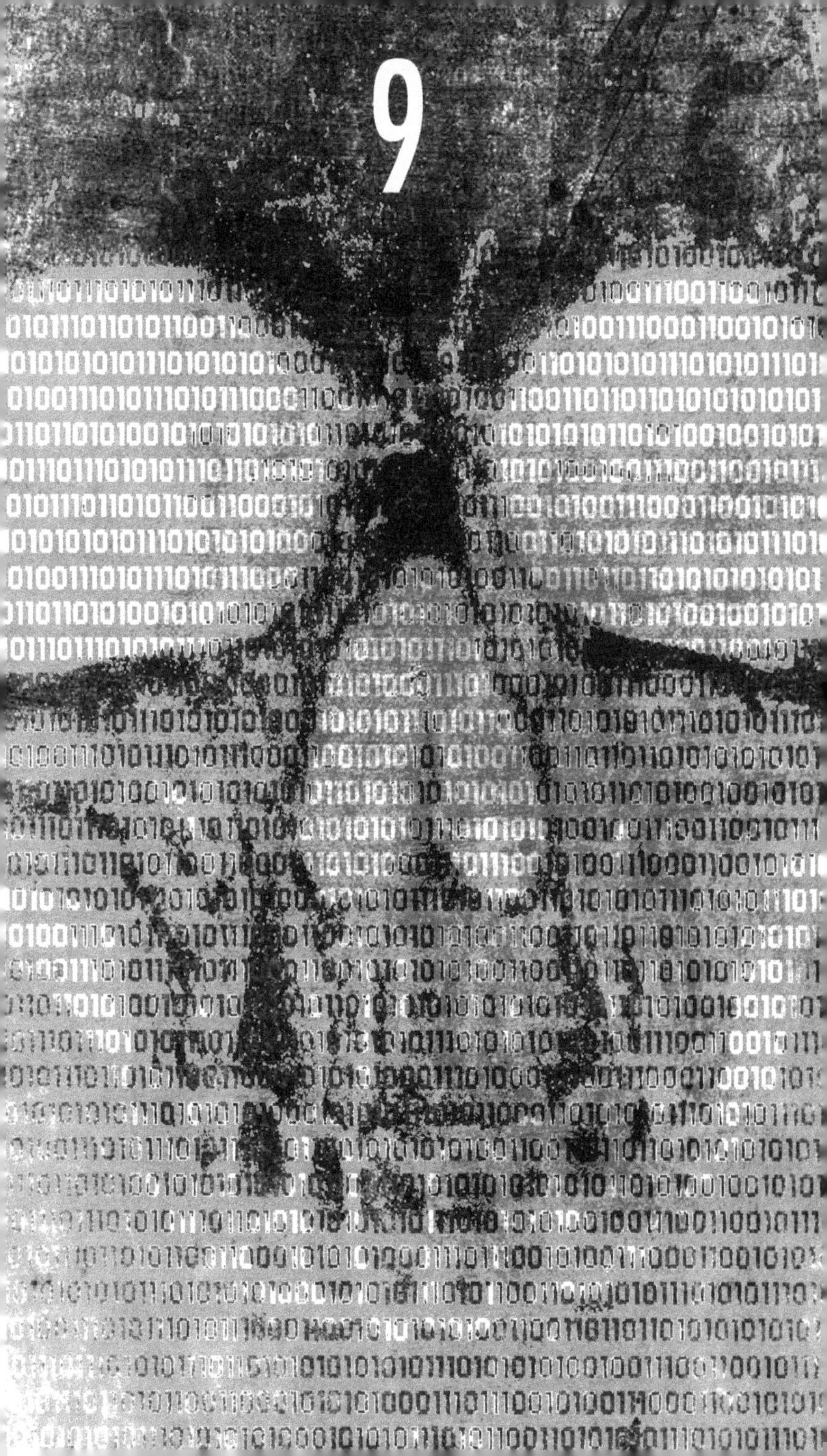
9

J. R. Park

It had been a long day but there was still work to be done. He had secured the flash drive with the Death's Head program and avoided capture from Royal and his men but it would not be long before they looked for him again. Unsure of his next move the one thing he knew for certain was that going back to his home was a bad idea. That would be the first place they would look. Mel had died just over three weeks ago and her family were still sorting out her belongings. Until that had been finalised it had been agreed that Norton would look after her house. Maybe it was just instinctive for him to come to this house whenever he needed help or comfort, but whatever the reason this was his hideout for the night. The added advantage was that Mel's house had a covered garage, a good place to hide the battered BMW.

'They'll have a tracking device on the car you know?' Orchid informed him. She was no longer in the police uniform that had previously been her disguise, but was dressed in prison overalls. They hung loosely from her toned physique. Her hands were still cuffed as she sat on a stool in the kitchen. The kitchen was large with a rustic design; its wooden shelves were full of crockery and tinned food. A fruit bowl sat proudly on the oak table, but it stood empty. The kitchen was clean but a layer of dust and dirt hung in the air and coated every surface. It looked like it hadn't been cleaned in weeks and the musty smell of inactivity seeped from the surroundings.

Orchid faced the backdoor; it was open and led to the garage. The garage was large enough to hold a car and works bench. Tools littered the bench and hung from the cold, cobwebbed walls of grey stone. Norton was in the garage scratching his head as he looked over the car.

'Where is it?' he asked.

'Uncuff me and I'll show you,' she said dryly knowing the response she was going to get before it came.

'I don't think so, you're far too dangerous for that.'

'Fine,' she huffed, 'go underneath the car. Check on the back left, near the axle.'

'Got it,' she heard him say, his voice becoming muffled as he climbed under the car.

'You have to be careful about removing-' her instruction was halted by the sound of a destructive bang. Orchid shuddered as she heard the sound and shook her head disapprovingly.

Norton entered the kitchen holding a hammer in one hand and a dented tracking device in the other.

'I've got it,' he said proudly. 'What did you say?'

'Never mind,' she replied rolling her eyes as she did so, 'now what are you going to do with it?'

Norton had already thought of that and took a piece of paper from the kitchen table. With quiet concentration he folded it with the skill of some practiced measure until he had constructed a paper boat and stuck the device to its base. Taking it outside he placed it on the river that flowed past the bottom of Mel's garden. He held it steady for a few moments to get the balance then let it go, watching it float off at speed down the river.

'I was going to suggest using a scrambler,' said Orchid when he returned back to the house.

'Sometimes the simple ways are the best,' he retorted.

'You call origami simple?' Orchid turned her attention back to the room and looked around. 'Where are we?' she asked.

'This is my girlfriend's house. Or at least was. She died. Recently,' his face saddened.

Orchid either didn't pick up on his change of mood or didn't care, either way she seemed to completely ignore it.

'I need to get out of this,' she looked down at her overalls. 'Can I borrow some clothes from here?'

'No!' Norton snapped.

'Sheeesh you are grumpy,' she said and turned away to look out the window into the garden.

Norton turned his back on her and stormed out of the kitchen. He stomped back to the garage, sitting down by the battered table strewn with tools. He put his hand in his coat pocket and pulled out the flash drive.

Eyeing it with curiosity he traced the scuffed edges of the writing.

What was he going to do with it? He thought about his many options. He should send them all down, leak it to the press and create a worldwide scandal. But the longer it was still around the more chance it had to fall into the wrong hands. If anyone in authority got hold of it then it would end up back with MI5. Give it to a journalist and they wouldn't be able to protect it against the likes of Orchid. He slowly began to wind round the handle of a vice that was bolted to the table, opening its metal jaws as he did so. How could something so small cause so much trouble? But the destruction it had caused; the deaths he had seen! It had to be destroyed; there was no way he could let it continue to exist.

He placed the flash drive into the jaws and began twisting the handle round and round. The turning action began to stiffen as the vice started to squeeze the piece of hardware. As he continued to close it the plastic casing split and squeaked before letting out a satisfying crunch as it cracked. The joy on hearing that sound did not make him stop in his work as he continued to crush the device. Round and round he continued to spin the handle. Closer and closer the jaws came together until they almost met. It had to be completely destroyed, until there was nothing left than dust. He stood to the side to get more leverage; propping one foot against the wall and, using all his strength, he pulled the vice as tight as it would go.

'There!' he said with an air of accomplishment.
'No!' Orchid screamed.

He turned round to see her stood in the garage, hands still cuffed behind her back but with a face twisted in anger.

'You stupid bastard!' she screamed as she kicked him in the chest and knocked him to the floor. 'You fucking stupid bastard! Fucking! Stupid!'

Orchid's verbal abuse was punctuated each time with a heavy boot to Norton's body. She continued to kick him whilst he laid, defenceless on the ground. He coughed blood as her foot buried into his stomach but unlike all the other times they had engaged in combat, this time he didn't fight back. Norton had achieved his aim and destroyed the threat of the Death's Head program, what was left here for him now? His career and reputation would be in ruins for going against MI5 and his only love had been brutally murdered. Every blow hurt, but he smiled with each impact hoping it could be the last bit of pain he would ever feel.

Orchid stopped her assault and put her foot on his chin, forcing his head back and exposing his neck. He closed his eyes, awaiting the end.

'Please,' he groaned, 'kill me.'

'I should kill you,' she said with disdain, 'but your miserable life seems punishment enough.'

He waited for the final blow. The final surge of pain as Orchid stamped on his windpipe and suffocated him.

But it did not come.

When Norton opened his eyes she was gone.

10

The soft, familiar feel to the sheets of Mel's bed hugged Norton with the reassurance of a lover. The morning sun was shining through the curtains giving the bedroom a comforting orange glow. He rolled over in a half waking slumber and felt the warmth of where Mel had been sleeping. Burying his head in the sheets he inhaled deeply allowing himself to absorb the beautiful, sweet scent of his girlfriend.

She's probably been up for hours, doing bits round the house, he thought.

The gentle clink of cutlery and china confirmed that she was making a cup of tea. It must be Saturday, he thought, she could never sleep in.

There'll be faint kisses on the lips next, he smiled; a nudge and then something like 'Come on lazy bones it's time to get up!' Then she'll probably rub my shoulders before resorting to my weak spot and tickle my feet.

He grinned to himself as he remembered the

last time that happened. She'd taken hold of his ankle and wiggled her fingers over the sole of his foot. He had roared with laughter and gently kicked his feet before grabbing her wrists. They'd wrestled on the bed and giggled; Mel had squealed with amusement as Norton managed to flip her on her back and pin her to the bed. They looked into each other's eyes and smiled before leaning closer. Their lips met, soft, fleshy and moist; the feeling of her lips on his sent a pulse of pleasure through his body. He felt the blood pump faster under his skin and a stirring in his groin as his penis began to swell. Her fingers gripped his erect cock as she slowly began to massage the shaft backwards and forwards, causing it to grow even larger in her palm. Mel bit her lip in anticipation of what was to come.

Norton's mobile began to ring and vibrated violently, pulling him from his half sleep.

He looked around and found he was in Mel's bed, but the room looked different. The cold, long shadows in the bedroom haunted a place that had been untouched for weeks. Certainly not touched by the hand of a house-proud owner, not by the hand of Mel. He reached across to Mel's side of the bed, it felt cold and empty. Around the room the long shadows held secrets; in the darkness there lingered the memories of love and smiles. Laughter, sex and happiness.

But they were only echoes; ripples from events that seemed so long ago.

He sat up in bed and looked around, the room bathed in a cold, blue morning light. He looked back at the tall, dark shadows that clung to the wall and concentrated on their centre, looking for the point of deepest black. Could that be a tunnel? A way to get back?

Norton turned his attention to a photograph on the bedside cabinet; it was a picture of himself and Mel. They were sat in a field with a picnic spread around them. The sun had been beautiful that day and he had surprised her by turning up at her doorstep with picnic food and a blanket. They drove out to the country, not knowing where they were going until they found an entrance to a quiet field and parked the car. It felt like their own world as they sat alone in the glorious sunshine amidst a beautiful countryside vista.

If only he could crawl into the photograph and back to that scene. To capture that time again.

The phone continued to ring and buzz impatiently.

Norton was still looking at the photograph.

Maybe if he believed really hard he could go back in time, he could. Maybe if he closed his eyes and concentrated on that time, on that place, the picnic, the feel of the sun on his skin, the sound of Mel's laugh as she practiced cartwheels in the field. Maybe he could open his eyes to find himself back there. Maybe if he closed them really, really tight and concentrated really, really hard.

Grief does stupid things to the mind. Hope warps expectation. When all realistic hope is gone people look towards the fantastical to keep those dreams alive.

But he wanted to believe so much.
So he closed his eyes.

He opened them again to find himself still alone in the
bedroom, rich with memories. His mobile phone
continued to ring and vibrate against the table. A tear
began to silently slide down his cheek. He picked up his
phone to turn it off. He needed to be alone right now.
Taking the device in his hand he looked at the screen.
The brightness of the display hurt his eyes and forced
them to squint. Through his compromised vision he
read the name of the incoming caller.

Mel.

He stopped breathing for a moment. His
stomach clenched, as he scarcely believed what he saw.
Had he done it? Had he been successful and managed
to go back through time? Did he somehow climb
through that photograph or journey into the darkest
patch of the shadow, emerging back in time to re-live
those sweetest of memories?

Nervously his finger went to press the *answer*
button. This could not be happening!

Thwak!

Just as his finger reached to press the screen his
phone was batted out of his hand and slid across the
floor. It skidded on the carpeted surface until it came to
a stop at the foot of the wardrobe; its vibration sounding
even louder as it amplified through the wardrobe's
acoustics. He turned to see Orchid standing beside the
bed. Her hands were no longer cuffed and she was no
longer adorned in the baggy cell clothes, instead she was
wearing the same coat, leggings and boots as on their

first encounter.

'That's Mel!' Norton spoke like a confused child.

'Don't be a fool, she's dead,' Orchid snapped, 'and we will be soon if you're not careful.'

'What's going on?' asked Norton. 'Am I dreaming?'

'Does this hurt?' Orchid hit him round the head with the palm of her hand.

'Ow! Yes!' Norton protested, rubbing his head.

'Fine, you're not dreaming,' Orchid was impatient in her tone. 'Get dressed and don't answer your phone. From here on in I am the only one you can trust.'

Norton got dressed in a state of bewilderment. He did not know what was happening and tried to piece everything together, but the shock of seeing Mel's number on his phone haunted him. The phone kept ringing with her number and he desperately wanted to answer it but it couldn't be her, could it?

'Leave that thing here,' Orchid said pointing to the incessantly noisy phone, 'or they'll trace us. Probably already have.'

'Orchid, what the hell is going on?' demanded Norton, now fully dressed and sat on the edge of his bed.

'We have to go!' she said.

'Go where? I'm not going anywhere until you tell me?'

Orchid sighed and acquiesced. She sat down on the bed next to him and explained. 'After I left you and slipped the cuffs some weird things started to happen. First of all my bank account had been frozen. That wasn't a problem as I have many accounts, however every time I used another one that was then frozen too. It was like the cash point was clocking my face then freezing my account. The CCTV cameras started to follow me. Now at first I thought I was being paranoid but then I heard rumours that the Death's Head program had been sent after me. I scanned police radio to discover they were claiming evidence had been found linking you to the deaths in the Areas building. I thought that was a bit weird so I came over to watch you. See what happened.'

'You slipped your cuffs?' Norton looked amazed. 'I'm a suspect for murder?'

'The cuffs? Yeah, it's not easy, but it is possible,' she began to look a little impatient again, 'and I thought it weird about the evidence. You don't look like a psycho murderer. That phone call. Isn't Mel your dead girlfriend?'

'Nicely put,' Norton replied.

'I'll make time for niceties when I'm not being hunted by a government funded computer program assassin. It seems like Royal and his men want our heads. Come with me, I know a man who can help us.'

Norton had suggested taking Royal's BMW, but Orchid rightly pointed out that the car would be spotted quite easily. Not only would they be looking for the number plate and model, the huge scratches down the sides from yesterday's chase made it rather conspicuous. She, on the other hand, had acquired a car this morning and changed its number plates. Norton looked at the white Porsche Boxster. He had to admire her work despite the bruises he had suffered from their previous encounters. They got in the car; Orchid started the engine and they drove off. Norton was a good detective and was used to putting pieces together but he didn't have all the facts to hand on this case. He continued to question Orchid who seemed more willing about giving information now they faced a common peril.

'I thought I'd destroyed the Death's Head program,' he asked as they drove through the city.

'You destroyed a copy of it,' Orchid answered, her eyes fixed on the road, 'that copy was downloaded onto the flash drive for a deal. Someone was selling it, but as you know it got…*lost*. That's why I was called in.'

'And it's after us?' he asked, as things began to become a little clearer.

'Seems so. Looks like Royal wants us dead.'

'So where are we going?'

'I like to research my targets and cargo,' Orchid admitted, 'I know more about the Death's Head program than I let on. Sure I told you a lot, but only enough to keep you interested so you'd hunt the thing out for me. Shame that plan backfired when you destroyed it.'

'You certainly let your feelings be known,' Norton softly stroked the bruises on his face.

'Sorry about that. I'm impulsive. You also lost me a lot of money.' She got back to her train of thought, 'I did some research on the program. It's amazing what you can find out with the right contacts, a bit of persuasion and a bit of hacking. Most importantly I found out who was responsible for the damn thing. I found out who the creator was and where he lives now. If anyone can help us he can.'

Orchid put her finger to an earpiece in her right ear. She strained to listen to the information that was coming through it.

'There are stop and searches all over the place,' she said. 'It's going to be a random route getting out of the city, but trust me.'

Using information from the police channel she was monitoring through her earpiece Orchid successfully navigated them out of the city limits and into the country. It had taken a good few hours but they were free, for now.

The lush, green landscape made for a beautiful view as they cruised along country roads.

'Ah, smell that,' said Orchid, her body relaxing now they had passed the threat of the stop and searches, 'good country air.'

Norton held his nose as his face screwed up, 'It smells of cow shit and grass. I thought country air was clean.'

'This is good honest air, Norton,' she said, her mood at ease for once. 'It's real. If there is shit at least it actually smells like shit. Not like in the city. Everything is false and pretending to be something it's not.'

'You're a country girl then?' he asked, intrigued to find out more about her.

She turned to face him and realised that perhaps she had given away more than she should. 'Most girls go through a horse phase,' she answered then turned back to face the road, her concentration back on the journey.

After nearly an hour of driving the roads had begun to look less and less like roads and more like forgotten dirt paths. Orchid turned off into a field and Norton had to ask:

'Is this even a road?'

'No,' came the short reply followed by, 'no cameras, no Internet, no phone signal. If you live here you really live here. Know what I mean, Norton?'

After a short drive across the field they came across a shack that stood in a rather pathetic condition at the base of a hill.

The shack was a crude affair made from corrugated metal sheets, rope and timber. It leaned slightly to one side and creaked in the wind. Outside a goat grazed on a patch of grass by the entrance, a rope from its neck led to a stake stuck firmly in the earth. Three chickens walked around pecking at the ground and to the side a small plantation of crops grew in a square of ploughed soil. An old man with a large, bushy, ginger beard sat on a crate, a make shift stool, and eyed the pair of strangers as they got out of their car and walked towards his home. His face was dirty, weathered and tanned; his skin was an off brown suggesting little in the way of washing. He wore a pair of dirty jeans that had turned a grey colour, a woolen, striped jumper and a battered straw hat. He rested a set of fingernails, thick with dirt, on the front of his hat and tilted it towards the oncoming visitors in a form of greeting.

'You've got to be kidding,' whispered Norton to Orchid as they made unsteady steps across the uneven surface of the field.

'Hello,' Orchid called out to the grubby stranger, 'are you Jon Newman?'

'Never heard of him,' the man replied.

The two approached the shack.

'Well there can't be many other people living out here,' Orchid said as she stood in front of the rural dweller, looking directly into his eyes. 'You are Jon Newman. You created the Death's Head program.'

'You must be lost,' said the old man, standing up to reveal a crooked posture.

'Mr Newman,' Orchid implored, 'we are being hunted by the program. I know it's you, I found your

116

details on the Security Services archives.'

Orchid held up a printed picture of the man wearing the same hat and beard outside of his own shack. It wasn't a posed portrait, but a photograph that had been taken during secret surveillance.

'It's a good likeness don't you think?' Orchid commented dryly.

'Oh god,' the man's face grew pale underneath the layers of mud, 'I knew they'd been watching me. But you can't just steal surveillance photos from their archives and not expect to be traced. No one's that good,' he shook his head in disbelief and annoyance. 'If they're after you, it wouldn't take a genius to work out you'd eventually end up here! You fools!'

Jon Newman looked up at the sky wildly like a meerkat checking for an unseen, airborne threat.

'Come inside quickly,' he waved them into the shack with panic and urgency in his voice.

Inside, the shack was orderly and well kept. Fur lined the walls and floor and a lamp burned in the centre. Jon took the burning lamp from the hook it was suspended from. He hurriedly moved a fur skin from the floor to reveal a trap door. Opening the door he motioned them in.

'Follow me,' he beckoned and disappeared down the hole.

Orchid and Norton followed to find a big narrow tunnel dug from the earth. It smelt damp as they caught up with Jon who was making a terrific pace down the passageway despite his crooked posture. Norton's large frame barely made it through, but it did and he pushed on, his shoulder's scraping the sides as he went.

'Keep moving,' shouted Jon to the two behind him. 'Do as I say and keep going!'

Suddenly the sound of a loud explosion was heard coming from above ground, the tunnel shook and bits of earth began to fall on their heads. Their pace quickened as they understood the threat. Behind him Norton heard a crash as part of the tunnel collapsed. There was no way back now.

'Keep moving,' yelled Jon over the noise of explosions that continued above ground, 'we'll hit the stronghold any minute.'

That news couldn't come soon enough. The tunnel behind Norton was collapsing and the avalanche of rock and earth was getting closer and closer. They ran as fast as they could on the unsteady surface of the tunnel, using their hands on the sidewalls to help stay upright. The tunnel opened up to a large room; this must be the stronghold! First Jon ran in, then Orchid. Norton felt the crumbling tunnel behind him as pieces of falling dirt began to roll down his neck. He ran and dived through the entrance of the room. Hearing a thud he looked behind to see Jon sealing the entrance with a solid metal door and bolt.

The sound of falling earth continued around them but the stronghold did not budge. A sense of protection came over them whilst they heard the storm of explosions from above ground. The lamp Jon carried offered some light in the gloom. As the light licked the edges of the stronghold Norton could make out its construction was formed of wielded pieces of solid metal, reaching from the floor to ceiling. It looked like a bomb shelter. Jon offered them crates to sit on whilst he fetched some water from a container in the corner of the room. As he did so the light of the lamp revealed a stockpile of tinned food next to the store of water. It was apparent that Jon had been prepared for something like this. Did he know he was going to be targeted, or was he just an end of the world crackpot that got lucky?

'Have a drink,' said Jon as he offered them both water from a cantina, 'you must be thirsty from all that running and crawling. We'll need to stay down here for a while. The explosions will have filled the tunnel in, there'll be no trace of that, but they'll be checking the area.'

'Who exactly are they?' questioned Norton.

'They are the people you are running from,' Jon replied as he sat down on an upturned crate, 'our very own country and government!'

They huddled round the light of the lamp in a circle staring into the burning flame. Norton reached out, putting his arm on Orchid's back he began to rub it gently. She relaxed back into the palm of his hand, enjoying the reassuring touch and closed her eyes.

In the darkness Jon began to open up, explaining all. Whether it was the fact that they had survived a near death experience, bringing them closer together, or whether it was the fact that he had seemingly lost everything and there was no longer any point hiding, Norton wasn't sure.

'They've been watching me for years,' Jon started, 'I'm no fool. But also I was no trouble out here, living a peaceful life off the land. You two coming along must have spooked them. Perhaps they wondered what would happen, so the best solution seemed to kill us. Kill us all in one hit.'

'So you did create the Death's Head program,' said Orchid, her eyes opening for the response then peacefully closing again, but still intently listening.

'Yes, yes I did,' Jon looked down at his feet; a sense of shame came over him, one that he had held for many years. 'It really was a clever invention. I was so wrapped up in the challenge and trying to improve it all the time that I lost sight of its practical application. To me it was all theory. A weapon that uses the enemies systems against them and then disappears without a trace. To begin with it was more akin to a weapon of mass destruction, hitting large bases and causing havoc, but I refined it. I also made it an assassin of almost unlimited knowledge and accessibly. No system could keep the Death's Head out of its information banks and that's one of the reasons why it is so deadly.

We are so reliant on technology as a civilization. A few lines of code are all it takes, a few megs of memory to hold all your details. Where you go shopping, what you buy, where you hang out. It's all traceable and trackable. All your messages about work or sent to loved ones, recorded and stored. From phones to email to social media. We all happily give this information and if you collate it all, you can track anyone, get to anyone.'

Orchid and Norton both sat up straight, beginning to feel ill at ease with what the ex-programmer was telling them.

He continued, 'In today's world everything we do is controlled by computers. We use computers to book a holiday, to pay our bills and do our shopping. From watching TV and looking for a new job to reporting a crime or registering a birth.

We no longer need to ask people in the street for directions let alone speak to our family or friends. We spend all day at work in front of a computer only to go home and do exactly the same in our free time.

Laptops, desktops, smart phones.

So many of us are hopelessly dependent on technology but very few of us understand how it works.

And all that information doesn't go anywhere. It just accumulates, building a detailed structure of our lives, understanding more about us than we do ourselves. From the mundane habits of where we buy our morning coffee to our deepest desires, recording all pornographic material we view, to the PIN numbers of our bank accounts. All that information is out there, on all of us, only guarded by bits of code and passwords.

In the past opposing armies would take geographical strong points, block trade routes and attack command buildings. In modern warfare the first thing you are going to hit are the computer infrastructures.

Take their secrets and disable their communications.

Nuclear and chemical weapons are no longer the biggest threat. In today's world the biggest weapon of mass destruction is simply a piece of computer coding.'

Jon looked at the other two, it was a long time since he'd talked to anyone about this and part of him was enjoying giving the explanation, 'Now if you set the Death's Head up with a target it can use face recognition to track you on CCTV cameras in streets and shops. It can even use the cameras built in to home computers provided they're connected to the internet. It can look at your purchases and bank statements, look for patterns of where you spend your money and when, then work out where you might be or are likely to show up.

It can hack into social media and look at your friends. It can then trace them to find you, or if that doesn't work it can put them in peril to bring you out of hiding. If it puts your mother in hospital chances are you will turn up there at some point. I'll admit it's sinister, but very clever.'

'This morning Detective Norton got a phone call from his dead girlfriend,' Orchid asked, 'do you think that had anything to do with the Death's Head program?'

'It's possible. If it was trying to find you it may have traced her via social media. It obviously hadn't crossed referenced its find with the death records, so maybe there are still a few bugs in the system. Either that or the records haven't been updated yet.' Jon drifted off in thought for a moment then came back, 'Careful about answering your phone. It can use it as a weapon just like it uses a computer.'

'Is there a way of tracing and destroying it?' Norton realised this was going to take more than a vice in a garage.

'You won't be able to trace it, no. It can move through all systems and deletes itself from them when finished leaving no impression behind. Utterly undetectable,' Jon looked up from the lamp, 'but there is a way to destroy it. Once they started testing the thing on real human subjects I realised what I had done. I didn't want to be a part of it, that's why I fled the city and moved here. I wanted to be as far away from a plug socket and telephone cable as I could get.

But before I left I created another program, an antivirus if you will, something to stop my terrible creation. Another clever piece of kit. It attracts the Death's Head program by pretending to be the target then sends out signals that the target has been killed. This in turn sets off the self-delete program in the Death's Head. The beauty of it is that once uploaded, and with a permanent web presence, it will eliminate this evil computer program forever. Each time they send it out this will wipe it. I called it the Flame.'

'Like a moth to the flame,' Norton thought out loud, 'very clever.'

'Very artistic,' mocked Orchid.

'We are all artists in our own little way,' mused Jon. 'There is nothing wrong with a flourish.'

'But why didn't you upload the Flame and rid the world of the Death's Head program?' quizzed Norton.

'It was a risk even trying to make it and go unnoticed. My plan was simple, to leave and don't bother them. That way I knew they'd leave me in peace. Which they did, up until now,' Jon stroked the curly knots of his beard.

Norton stood up to stretch his legs. 'Do you have the Flame?' he asked.

'No I entrusted it to my nephew. He's a simple

lad, but with a good heart. He doesn't even know he has it,' the stroking motion on Jon's beard became much slower as he gave up the secret he had never let pass his lips before. 'During my years in research I found the best form of secret keeper is one totally unaware they have a secret to keep.'

'I knew it!' Orchid rose to her feet in excitement. 'I knew he had something to do with it!'

'You know him?' Norton looked surprised by her sudden outburst.

'Gregory Light. I found him when I hunted through Jon's files,' Orchid explained. 'There was no proof or evidence to link him other than the family connection, but I just knew there was something there. I've been searching his flat for weeks!'

Suddenly it dawned on Norton, 'Gregory Light? Mr Light?!' He stuttered as he made the words form in his mouth, 'You're the stalker? With the impossibly long legs?'

The description fits, he thought, as he sat back on the crate and chuckled to himself.

They needed a plan, and as they sat discussing it in the dimly lit bunker, waiting for a safe time to leave, one began to form.

12

If it weren't for the watches they wore, they would have lost track of time hidden in the bunker, the stronghold that Jon had built under his shack. He had feared an attack from someone; you don't work so closely with the most advanced and potentially damaging weapons system and not come into contact with people that would rather have you dead. His fears had been founded and his escape plan had worked well. It wasn't until twelve hours had passed that he felt it was safe to show his two visitors the way out. The search parties of their aggressors would have seen the devastation and when they had not found any bodies or people trying to flee they would have assumed they were successful. That level of bombing would have burnt away most corpses. What was left would be hard to differentiate between animal flesh and human flesh after it was splattered into tiny pieces of charred matter. Jon felt sorry for the loss of his animals, but during his time living in the countryside he had developed a new found understanding and closer relationship with nature. He respected death and was philosophical about the need for change in whatever form it took.

When the time was right he guided the detective and the mercenary out through a reinforced shaft that was hidden on the other side of the room. The shaft had been far enough away to escape the majority of the explosive forces; the minor shockwaves it had felt were withstood by the metal casing Jon had spent months secretly work on.

It wasn't an easy route back to the surface as the foliage around the exit had been allowed to grow wild in order to conceal itself on the side of the hill. The plan had worked enough to fool their would-be killers, but it did mean an extra thirty minutes of hacking, slashing and pulling. Jon always carried a small knife with him, but was pleased, as well as surprised, that the beautiful Japanese lady had a pair of much larger knives with her. They made short work of the vegetation that prevented their escape, and it would have taken a few more hours had she not been with them.

By the time they left the tunnel it was dark and around two in the morning. Thankfully the new moon meant they had as much chance of going undetected as possible.

Jon's philosophical nature did not change when they arrived back at the remains of the shack. Pieces of sheet metal, wood and feathers were scattered amidst impact craters from where the bombs had hit.

'They certainly weren't taking any chances,' said Jon as he surveyed the site, one hand holding his hat, the other scratching his head.

'I'm sorry Jon,' Orchid spoke softly and sympathetically.

'Oh don't worry about it,' he said strangely chipper, 'it's dry and warm. I'll rebuild. It's the way of things. Besides I was getting sick of the view. Time to move on anyway.'

Orchid and Norton said their goodbyes and set off on the walk back to the main road. As they left, Norton looked back, envious of Jon's freedom and his easy manner in which he dealt with loss.

'It's a long walk back then,' Norton pointed out as they walked past a smouldering crater full of rubble where once Orchid's newly acquired Porsche stood.

'Yeah it's a long way all right,' sighed Orchid.

They were a mis-matched pair as they walked along the road; hitch hiking their way back to the city. The journey took them hours and conversation cropped up between them as a means to keep them both motivated and entertained.

'So how long have you been following Mr Light?' Norton had to ask after the revelation in the bunker.

'I was keeping him under surveillance for a couple of weeks,' she replied as they slowly walked along the side of the road, 'watching his movements and searching his belongings.'

'And his underwear drawer?' Norton chuckled as he said it.

'You have to be thorough!' she protested, laughing and scowling at him in equal measure.

She looked at him and smiled, he smiled back.

'How did you know it was him you had to follow,' Norton returned back to the conversation in hand.

'I did a check on Newman's family connections and searched them all,' she explained, 'but Light was different. I couldn't find any dirt on him but something bugged me, I just knew…' she trailed off for a moment, 'Call it intuition, a feeling, but I knew he was connected. That's something a computer can't pick up on.'

The sun began to rise, revealing a landscape of lush fields covering gently rising hills like a patchwork cloth, separated by thick hedges. With it, the warmth began to thaw the ground and their toes. They held their thumbs out as cars drove by hoping a kind soul would take them back to the city.

'This saving the world stuff is glamorous work,' joked Norton as they trudged on.

'Sure is,' came the reply from a weary Orchid.

By the time they got back to the city via a few friendly drivers the day was in full swing. Jon had filled them in on the types of dangers to watch out for. It was imperative to only use cash to buy things, no electronic trace, he had warned. They bought hats and long coats so as to avoid their faces being caught on CCTV as much as they could. The Death's Head program would be monitoring the cities security cameras, running facial recognition programs on each person it viewed in order to find them. They tried to avoid streets with cameras on all together, making their route to Mr Light's apartment via back alleys. These streets were left unprotected, a place where the dregs of society could be free from the watchful eye of the authorities. This was the dwelling place of the homeless, the hooker, the drug dealer and the daytime drinker. A place you'd find the banker looking for a cheap thrill. This was where all the unwatched go to live their lives in freedom.

Norton wondered as he made his way through this landscape with a wanted hit woman why the law-abiding citizens couldn't be granted this kind of privacy?

'This is the back of Ashgate Place. Mr Light's flat is up there,' Orchid informed him as she opened the metal cage door that led to the rusty fire escape which zig-zagged up the building, 'number sixteen.'

Norton followed her up as she counted the floors. They got to the fourth floor then she stopped and opened the fire door. They made their way along the hall to the entrance of Mr Light's flat.

'He's not in,' she said confidently, 'he's always out until eleven.'

Norton took a run up at the door and rammed his shoulder hard against it. He bounced off whilst the door stayed firmly in place. He rubbed his shoulder; the bruising from all those fights had taken its toll and this building had better landlords.

'He also never locks his door,' Orchid smiled and turned the handle, gently opening the door.

The flat was tidy and bright. The sun shone through the windows, casting a beam of light onto a coffee table that took centre place in the middle of the room.

'Right, we need to get looking,' said Norton.

'You handle in here,' Orchid pointed at the bookcase in the living room, 'and I'll handle in there,' she pointed to the bedroom.

They searched the flat for an hour but could not find anything. It wasn't a large dwelling with only a hallway, a living room, a small kitchen, a smaller bathroom and a bedroom.

'The problem is,' Norton huffed in frustration, 'I don't really know what I'm looking for.'

'Jon said look for the Flame, it will be obvious,' Orchid's voice showed signs of equal frustration.

'Jon Newman is a crackpot living in the country,' he sighed. 'We don't even know if he really invented the Flame or the Death's Head program. He could have been spouting a load of horse shit for all we know.'

Their argument was cut short when the door handle to the front of the flat began to squeak as it turned. Someone was coming in!

Gregory Light had just come back from his morning walk around town. It was a sunny day and he'd stopped to watch the water dance in the fountains by the Hengrove Hotel. He liked the way the ripples and reflections of light seemed to move together. He hadn't gone far as it took him a while to walk anywhere now a days; his leg seemed to be getting worse. He put his keys on the coffee table and felt the warmth of the sunrays beam through his window.

The last few days had been peaceful. He hadn't seen hide nor hair of the Asian woman that had been following him around recently. He'd half expected to see her behind every door he opened, but those notions had slowly faded since his last sighting. It seemed she had given up.

He opened his bedroom door and quickly realised he had been very wrong about that.

On his bed lay the same beautiful woman. She was dressed only in a lacy, black bra and thong. His eyes followed the curves of her bosom, then traced the hourglass turn of her stomach and hips. She suggestively parted her legs and he watched as she slid her hand down her silky thigh, leaving it to rest on the warm, lace underwear that covered her crotch. She gently stroked herself playfully with her fingertips and with perfect, full lips she whispered, 'Where have you been?'

Orchid got to her hands and knees and slowly crawled across the bed towards him. She took him by the shoulders and with surprising strength pulled him onto the bed. She lay back and guided him on top of her, instantly feeling his erection poking her thigh through his trousers.

Orchid looked over Light's shoulder to where Norton was hiding behind the door. She mouthed the words *now* and *help me*, but was only met with a cheeky smile and an okay sign.

Fearing to break the pretence she carried on and pushed his head between her breasts. His tongue licked against her bosom as his fingers began to slide up her thigh.

'All right sunshine, that's enough,' Norton's voice came booming from behind him and instantly the pair froze.

'Thank God,' Orchid cursed as she got up from the bed and threw a piece of rope toward Norton. 'Tie him up. I'm going to put my clothes back on.'

Norton tied Mr Light securely to a chair he had taken from the kitchen and began to question him. The bald man looked confused and said he knew nothing about any Flame, and neither had he seen Uncle Jon in years. Constant questioning yielded the same answers.

The two captors walked back into the living room and shut the bedroom door; they didn't want him to hear their conversation.

'Well it's obvious he doesn't know anything,' Norton said pacing the room.

Orchid sat on the sofa, dejected and in agreement, 'So what are we going to do?' she said. 'We can't leave him like that!'

'I don't know,' Norton idly looked out the window searching for inspiration amongst the pedestrians walking below.

'It has to be here,' Orchid held her head in her hands and talked at the floor.

'Does it?' replied Norton, his gaze lost to the moving throng of people outside. 'It doesn't have to be anywhere. It doesn't have to exist. Why didn't Jon just tell us out right where it was?'

'He was paranoid, and had every right to be,' Orchid grew impatient with Norton questioning the only lead they had. 'He felt honest and I trust my hunches. They've done me pretty well so far.'

'Well it's not helping right now with Jon's bloody riddle is it?' Norton turned from the window and faced his make shift companion. 'Look towards the light and you'll see the flame,' he quoted.

'This is Light's flat I get that bit,' Orchid's voice became strained.

'Crock of shit,' Norton huffed, 'I'm sick and tired of looking at that man.'

'But this is the only bit of hope we've got-' Orchid was cut off mid-sentence by a noise from another room.

Clunk!

The noise came from the bedroom. Norton and Orchid looked at each other for answers but neither had any. Immediately realising this they both ran to the source of the sound and where their prisoner was held. They found Mr Light still tied to the chair but laid on his side, his face squashed into the carpet where he fell. Next to him was a mobile phone, the screen was illuminated and the caller number was visible: it read 999. A voice could be heard coming from the speaker.

'Hello?' the voice said from the phone. 'Hello? Are you there? We have traced you from your mobile and we'll be sending a police car over. Please respond if you are there.'

'Shit,' cried Orchid as she picked up the phone and turned it off.

'We've got about fifteen minutes tops to get out of here,' said Norton as he looked at his watch.

'Why did you do that?' Orchid spoke to Mr Light as she crouched down next to him.

As the simple man lay helpless on the floor Orchid noticed a chain around his neck. She pulled it out from his shirt and attached to it she saw a silver pendant in the shape of fire. Hoping she was right Orchid examined the pendant further and found she

could slide up the back panel revealing a USB connector.
It was the Flame.

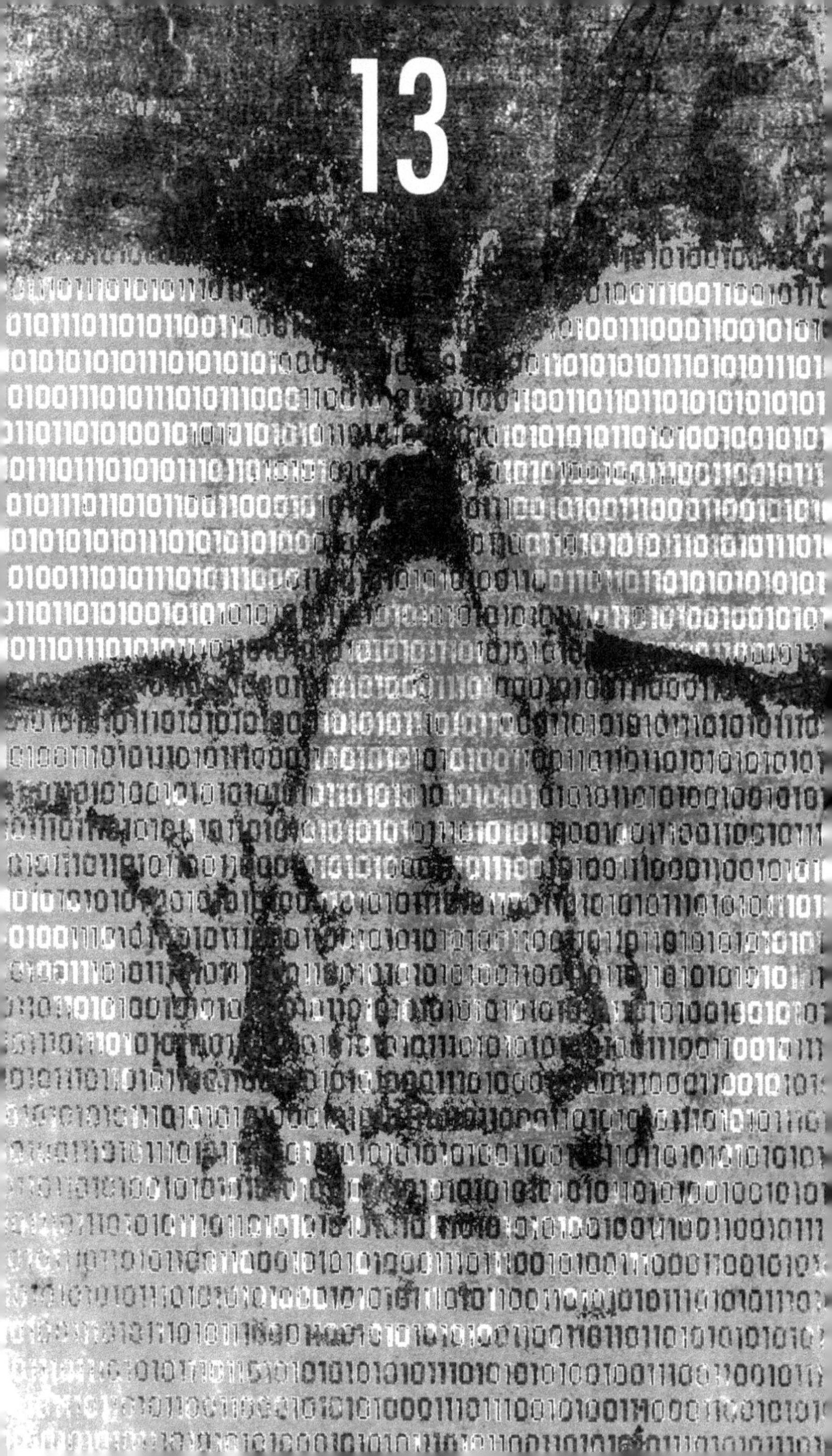
13

Norton and Orchid bolted down the fire escape, the Flame safely tucked into one of Orchid's pockets. Mr Light did not have a computer in his flat so they needed somewhere with Internet access where they could plug the USB in, release the antivirus and put an end to the computer generated threat.

'Damn it, we've been spotted,' cried Orchid as she pointed down the street.

A police car had pulled up answering the 999 call. Orchid had seen the young constable emerge from his car and immediately clocked them running down the fire escape. He was talking into his radio in a matter of seconds. With Norton and Orchid's names mentioned down the airwaves it wouldn't be long before every uniformed patrol was out looking for them along with Royal and his men from the MI5.

'No use trying to hide now,' she said as they reached street level.

To Norton's surprise Orchid ran towards the

police car, not away. He tried to call her to stop but had learnt that asking Orchid what she was doing was a question that would mostly be treated with contempt. He ran after her thinking it was too late now to split up; they were well and truly in this together.

PC Andrews had got out of his car and gripped his canister of PAVA spray as Orchid and Detective Norton came charging towards him. She was as pretty in real life as the photo they'd all been given yesterday in the brief, but that wasn't any comfort when he was alone and faced two of the cities most wanted people.

Orchid ran towards him; Andrews held his PAVA and sprayed but missed her completely. Orchid had leapt on to the bonnet of his squad Hyundai and vaulted over his head in a somersault avoiding the incapacitating spray. She landed behind him and with a swift kick to the back of his knees PC Andrews was brought to the ground with a cry of pain.

Norton caught up with the pair to find Orchid holding a knife to the police constable's throat.

'I'm sorry Andrews,' the detective sounded genuinely apologetic in his tone, 'give me the keys and we'll be on our way.'

Andrews nodded gently and with a hand trembling in fear, he took the keys to the Hyundai from his pocket and handed them to Norton. The big detective took the keys as the sound of rotor blades began to thunder through the air. Looking up they saw a police helicopter hovering above them.

'Damn it,' shouted Norton over the noise as he jumped into the car, 'let's go.'

Orchid got into the passenger side and Norton

fired up the engine. As he pulled away he could hear the sound of sirens coming up the road from behind. He turned the sirens on in their car hoping to draw the others off their scent with some confusion but he knew it wouldn't work against the astute cops. They would be taking intel from the helicopter that was watching their every move.

'Where are we going?' it was Orchid's turn to ask the questions.

'I don't know,' came the uncomforting response.

They drove through the city weaving in and out of the traffic as their pursers began to gain on them. The radio in the car had been full of details about their chase when something else caught Norton's ear.

'There have been reports of two pile-ups in the centre. Both seem to be connected with malfunctioning traffic lights,' the radio announced.

The police cars drew ever closer as Norton shouted across to Orchid, 'Didn't Jon say something about the Death's Head program controlling all the systems? It's messing up the traffic lights. It's trying to build road blocks to trap us.'

Another police car appeared in front of them from a side road, attempting to obstruct their path. Norton violently turned the car a sharp left, the tyres screeched as they struggled to keep their grip on the tarmac.

'They're gaining on us Norton, we've got to get off this road,' Orchid looked out the back window at the police cars as one of them came close and nudged their bumper causing them to lurch forward. 'That chopper has us pinned even if we shake this lot.'

The nudge had made them swerve violently; losing speed, two squad cars were able to catch them and drove side by side with Norton and Orchid; keeping them contained in a vehicle sandwich. Norton swung his car to the left, then to the right, trying to knock them off their path and give himself some room but they did not budge and resolutely held their line. They approached a crossroads, three lanes each way, controlled by traffic lights. He hoped the traffic lights would hold them up and force the other two away from his sides but the traffic started to move freely. Instantly Norton could see what was happening but was powerless to do anything about it. The traffic lights from all directions had switched to green, presumably by the Death's Head program in an attempt to kill them in an accident, or at the very least stop them. The traffic all drove forward heading towards each other. Norton was surrounded by police cars with no possible way to deviate from his forward path. To stop would mean immediate capture. He would have to roll the dice this time and see where his luck lay.

'Hold on tight,' he warned Orchid as he continued driving into the crossroads.

The first lot of cars that were pulling away from stationary positions were able to see each other and stop before a collision, sounding a tirade of abusive horns and hand signals. The following cars behind were not so lucky; arriving at a greater speed it was harder to stop and they careered into the blockage of traffic ahead. Each car slammed into the next as glass showered across the street. Norton collided with the car in front, coming to an immediate halt and felt the police cars that were on either side smash against his left and right. They had both taken an impact from cars coming in other directions on the crossroads. Luck had been on his side; the two police cars had absorbed the impact of the oncoming traffic, protecting him and his companion. The two officers were dazed but did not look badly hurt. Norton looked over to Orchid who seemed a little shaken but not in any pain. She gave a thumbs up, signaling she was okay, before ejecting her seat belt.

They both climbed out of the wreckage and into the carnage around them.

In a state of blind panic they ran across the road to see police car after police car arrive on the scene. Diving into the nearest building for cover they caught their breath and a strange sense of déjà vu hit them.

'Happy anniversary,' Orchid said between gasps.

'Huh?' Norton quizzed.

'We are back where we first met,' she pointed out. 'This is the Areas building.'

Mayhem reigned outside the Areas building. Fire engines arrived to cut survivors from the wreckage of their cars whilst ambulances waited to treat the injured. Sirens sounded and lights flashed red and blue against the scene of the accident. A number of police cars had pulled up outside the building and were ignoring the scene behind them; they had matters to deal with inside. The police officers stood outside in a group discussing what had just happened whilst the helicopter hovered overhead. Three black BMWs pulled up alongside them. From the cars, out stepped men dressed in well tailored suits.

'Stand down blue,' said Royal to the police as he got out of one of the cars, 'this is ours. Keep a perimeter. Let no one in.'

Norton looked around the lobby and recognised it. Orchid was right. He noticed the security camera on the wall was pointed directly at them. They moved towards the lifts and the camera moved too, following them as they walked.

'Don't take the lifts,' he warned, 'it looks like the Death's Head program is here.'

The lights flickered and went down, leaving the lobby dimly lit with only the overcast day as illumination. A monitor by the lifts began to flicker and the usual display of the lobby area via the security camera began to disappear in static. The image throbbed on the screen until it twisted itself into a skull made of the same hissing static. The display then began to flash in near blinding bright strobes.

'Don't look at it,' Orchid said as she took a knife from her pocket and threw it at the monitor. The blade flew through the air with confident precision and pierced the glass; the display spluttered for a moment then disappeared.

As the picture faded a high-pitched noise began to emit from the monitor's speakers. The frequency seemed to seep into their brains and they both held their ears in pain. Norton motioned toward a door and they ran through it, finding themselves in a stairwell. The stairwell was devoid of electronic equipment and the door offered some protection from the deadly sound.

For the moment they were safe but they knew it wouldn't last.

'Here,' said Orchid passing Norton some ear plugs she took from a pouch on her belt, 'they won't offer much protection, but something is better than nothing.'

He put them in his pocket as they ran up the stairs. The ground floor door burst open amid a fury of gunfire that just missed them. Royal's men had arrived and were giving chase.

Orchid and Norton exited the stairwell onto the next floor and into a busy office. The workers all stopped to look at the two as they burst through the door.

'I'm a cop,' screamed Norton, 'get out of here now, your lives are in danger.'

The office panicked as the sound of gunshots echoed from the stairwell. The crowd of workers ran through the doors like a herd of scared cows, blindly running to any exit. Gunshots sounded in the office as an MI5 agent fought through the terrified crowd that were fleeing down the stairs and burst through the door. Diving behind desks for cover the wanted pair hid from the agent and his searching gun.

Norton crouched behind a desk, his big frame barely hidden by the furniture. Orchid was hiding behind another desk across the office.

Getting her attention Norton looked to her and whispered, 'Get that drive into a computer.'

Orchid took the Flame out of her pocket and put her head above the desktop to find the computer terminal. A shot fired off making a hole in the computer and narrowly missing Orchid. She instantly ducked back down for cover.

She turned to Norton, 'I can't!'

The screens began to flicker and the same evil, static skull they had seen before appeared on all the monitors in the office. A high-pitched whine started to sound from the speakers of the computers, sending the mercenary, the detective and the MI5 agent to floor in agony. They rolled around trying to block the sound with their hands and find a way out of the room.

Norton and Orchid rammed their earplugs into their ears. As Orchid had suggested it didn't block the noise out completely but it offered some level of protection against the higher end of the frequencies. The MI5 agent was not so prepared and lay on the floor screaming in pain, his sounds of anguish drowned out by the sonic attack of the Death's Head program. He began to convulse and spasm as blood trickled from his ear. As he fitted on the floor death was not far away.

Orchid rolled against a wall and noticed a printer next to her. Crawling towards the large grey contraption she opened a drawer in its base and pulled out sheets of paper. Scrunching them into balls she took a lighter from her pocket and set them on fire. The paper ignited quickly, producing a large orange flame. The heat and smoke wafted to the ceiling, setting off the fire sensors. A loud alarm rang over the top of the din and water rained down on the office from the sprinklers above. The water soaked everything in the office as the sprinklers released their liquid load. An electrical spark ignited from one of the plug sockets, its bright flash lit the room up for a moment then all of a sudden everything went dark. The alarm continued to ring but the pain had stopped in their heads; the sonic attack had ceased.

'It can't touch us when there is no electricity,' Orchid smiled.

They ran out of the office into the first floor lift lobby. The electricity was still working out here but the lights flickered as if the building itself was mortally wounded. Shots fired again as Royal and one of his men emerged from the stairwell. Instinctively they bolted in the other direction.

'No,' Norton shouted, 'we're in the lift, we have to get out of here!'

In their panic to avoid the gunshots they had dived into one of the lift cars! A static hiss came over the speakers and the doors began to close. They both made a dash to escape the possessed car but were knocked back by one of Royal's men. He was damned if he was going to let them get away. His over eagerness did not pay off as the closing doors caught him, trapped halfway. Unable to move he was stuck between the doors, pinched by two metal panels. Normally the lift sensors would have detected a blockage and opened again but this lift was not following its normal operating procedure, it was under the control of the Death's Head program. The doors began to squeeze together, harder and harder like a vice. The agent screamed in pain as slowly he was crushed, the sound of his bones snapping echoed in the confines of the lift car.

'*Going up,*' came the recorded voice over the tannoy.

Realising what was happening the agent

screamed louder, begging for help. The lift began to move gradually upwards pulling the agent with it. Norton and Orchid reached out toward the agent and tried to pull him free but the doors held him too tightly. The car ascended and his head hit the ceiling of floor one as he tried desperately, but unsuccessfully, to escape. His head and neck were pushed, inch-by-inch closer together whilst the bones of his legs broke at the knees as he tried in vain to stand tall against the force of the lift. Cartilage tore with a horrifying sound and bone ripped the skin, protruding from his thigh amid a spray of blood. His body seemed to compact down, as one by one his ribs were crushed together. Like a tube of toothpaste his body was squeezed from the bottom up. They heard his neck snap. His head hung lifeless as his internal organs began to flow from his mouth, being forced out by the moving car. Within a few minutes all that was left was a pinkish pile of broken bones, blood and guts. The lift doors were free to close and a puddle of gore sloshed on the car floor.

The lift continued up for a while longer then it stopped.

They looked at each other, sprayed in blood and stunned from the scenes they had witnessed.

Norton broke their shocked silence, 'We must be at the top of the building.'

Slowly they felt themselves began to descend. The lift car shook and shuddered as it began to pick up speed. Faster and faster the lift traveled as it plummeted downwards. Norton had seen the mess this had made to an unlucky couple earlier in the week and held out no hope for survival. All ideas escaped him except one. He leaned forward and put his arms round Orchid pulling her close to him. Her arms reciprocated the tender action as they held each other; eyes closed tight, waiting for the moment of impact.

J. R. Park

14

J. R. Park

The moment of impact never came. At least, not like they thought it would. The lift car jolted and suddenly stopped. Everything went black and they fell to the gore soaked floor, but despite a bit of bruising they were uninjured.

Getting to his feet Norton assessed the situation. 'We didn't pick up enough speed or drop far enough. We never hit the bottom,' his voice elated with joy to have survived, 'the power's gone out in the lift shaft. The sprinklers must have shorted it. Death's Head can't get to us.'

'But where are we?' asked Orchid.

'Somewhere between floors, if I can just get the door open,' Norton answered as he took hold of the edge of one door panel.

With his foot against the wall to help as leverage Norton used his brute strength to prise the door open. It was slow going but inch-by-inch he managed to pull it apart, enough for them to climb out. He got to his knees and looked down the gloomy shaft.

'I can see some light a few feet down,' he said peering between the car and the shaft wall. 'It looks like the doors have been opened. If we can climb down we should be able to swing across.'

They hadn't decided who was going to try their luck first when a thud came from above them. The car rocked from side to side throwing them against the walls. When the rocking died down they heard knocking above their heads. Were they footsteps?

'Like a pair of sitting ducks!' Royal's voice came booming through the shaft as he paced the roof of the lift car. 'You captured yourselves! Perfect!'

He laughed hysterically, his voice sounded ragged, like a man on the edge. The confines of the lift shaft amplified his speech giving him the menace of a vengeful god. He drew his gun and wildly shot through the ceiling, forcing the captive pair to cower.

'Having fun in there?' Royal shrieked like a mad man.

'Royal you crazy fool!' Norton shouted back.

More shots fired down through the ceiling. Orchid yelled in pain as a bullet hit her calf muscle, tearing a hole clean through the flesh and out the other side. She fell to floor clutching her leg and gritted her teeth. The MI5 man was right; they were like sitting ducks in there.

'I'm not playing around!' Royal screamed in anger.

He opened a hatch in the ceiling and looked down at his prey. Orchid lay on the floor holding her bleeding leg whilst Norton knelt beside her. They both looked up to see the wild, staring eyes of Royal. Gone was the cool, calmness Norton had witnessed in the blood soaked flat of George the unlucky IT worker. The control with which Royal conducted himself had seemed frightening with its efficiency but this had been replaced by an altogether more terrifying mania. Royal paced backwards and forwards on the roof of their makeshift cell, never once taking his eyes off his two prisoners.

'I went looking for you,' he shouted down with his gun trained on them both. 'I went to your dead girlfriend's house. I found a lot of unpleasant dust and smashed plastic in the garage. Just enough to be a smashed up flash drive. Don't tell me you've destroyed it Norton?' He continued with his speech, not caring for an answer, 'I wanted that stick. That was going to set me up for life. Do you know how hard it was for me to get that smuggled out of the agency? Do you?!'

He stopped pacing and squatted down next to the edge of the hatch, fixing them with a crazy grin.

'Everything is locked down so tightly at the agency that it took a year of planning to smuggle that out. I was so careful, so meticulous. If you did smash it up and you no longer have it,' he shrugged, 'I'm going to have to kill you.'

'We couldn't throw away something so valuable,' Norton lied. 'I have it here.'

'Good,' Royal almost purred his words with happiness, 'I don't want to lose it again.'

Like Jon Newman, Royal seemed to be happy to talk and wandered off track as if he had been desperate to tell someone of his successes and woes. To share tales that had been pent up inside for so long.

'I lost it before; so stupid. How carefully one sets up a meeting and plans for every eventuality, every possible mishap. Except the common mugger. He took me by surprise; left me out cold on the floor and took my bag; he took the flash drive.' Royal looked up along the darkened lift shaft and continued his monologue to his captive audience. 'An unfortunate fellow that mugger, he had no idea of the value of that flash drive. He just threw it away. Of course we didn't know at the time. I had him followed. We questioned him but he didn't let on about its whereabouts. I thought he was bluffing, but I needed to be sure so I pushed him. He was a criminal, sure, but he wasn't mad, not until I sent the Death's Head after him. I thought if we got him scared he'd come running to us for help and give me back that which he stole.

We didn't know he was going to flip out as bad as he did.

And it was an unfortunate turn that he offed your girlfriend, Norton, but there are always casualties.'

Norton's anger boiled over when he heard this. If what he said was true, then the agency man was as responsible for Mel's death as if he had pulled the trigger himself. Enraged, the detective leapt up and took a swing at Royal above him. The MI5 agent recoiled backwards, avoiding the large fist and fired a warning shot across the car. Norton jumped back, simmering with fury.

'You bastard,' Norton swore through gritted teeth.

'Shut your moaning mouth and give me the

stick before I shoot both of you,' Royal demanded, leaning forward and holding out his hand.

At that moment the power flickered on briefly, the lights flashed and the lift car shot down a few feet, before stopping again, plunging them back into darkness. Norton took that moment and grabbed Royal's hand, shaking the gun from his grip and pulling him into the car. The lights began to flicker again.

'Get out the lift,' shouted Norton, 'it looks like the power is coming back on!'

The car had fallen in line with the doorway Norton had previously spied below them. Taking the moment whilst it presented itself they all ran out of the lift, getting to the safety of the office floor just in time to see the car plummet to the ground.

The three stood alone in an empty, harshly illuminated office. Computer monitors sat on top of each desk and the screens began to flicker in unison. They began to flash as the twisted skull of static appeared in the centre of each one. The Death's Head program had them back where it wanted and now it was going to eliminate its targets, regardless of who else it took out in the process. The computers started to make a crackling noise that quickly turned into the deadly, high-pitched sonic attack. Orchid and Norton dived on to the floor to avoid the flashing lights and jammed their earplugs back in their ears. Royal looked around, not knowing what to do. He cupped his ears trying to block out the sound, but the whine penetrated his make shift protection and his head pulsated with pain.

He dropped to his knees and tried to scream but was silenced by the contents of his stomach erupting out through his mouth. He retched and retched, unable to stop the flow of bile and semi-digested chunks of food from being forced up from his gut and onto the floor. Unable to catch his breath the uncontrollable heaving was causing him to suffocate. He flailed his arms around in a desperate attempt to find something that would aid him.

'Help me,' came a pathetic and desperate cry for help from the MI5 man.

In mid swing his fingers caught the wire of a monitor. He pulled at it wildly bringing the monitor and its attached computer crashing down on his head. The weight of the heavy hardware caught him full and he collapsed to the floor; his face was badly cut from the impact and blood poured from deep gashes. As he fell to ground he began to shake violently. In pain he let out a scream, but another seizure forced his jaw shut causing his teeth to sink into his tongue, biting through the soft flesh. He opened his mouth again releasing a torrent of blood that poured from this horrific wound. His skin grew pale as slowly, life drained from his weakened and wretched frame.

Orchid could see Norton curled up in a fetal position. His back was facing her so she couldn't work out if he was alive; if he was then he was surely in pain. Her head throbbed and her eyes watered as the sound affected her balance. She tried to stand but it was like they were at sea in a terrible storm. The floor seemed to rock violently up and down and side to side. She gritted her teeth and fumbled around in her pocket searching for something. She prayed she hadn't lost the Flame. It must be here. At last her fingers found the disguised

USB stick, the seemingly innocent charm that had held a secret for so many years. Holding on to the edge of a desk she pulled herself up trying to keep her vision away from the strobing lights that flashed wildly from the screens. Using her hands as a guide she thumbed a computer and through her touch she found a USB socket. The sonics increased in pitch and she began to heave as her stomach tightened in response to the disorienting sound. Orchid pushed the Flame into the USB socket and hit the enter key to run the program. She collapsed on the floor, all her effort now spent, and prayed it had worked.

The screen began to flash a red colour.

The strobes stopped and all the screens began to display the same message.

Target located.

Verifying............

......target eliminated...........

The noise ceased and the static skull that hung in the centre of the screens began to melt away, piece by piece, returning their displays back to normal.

The Flame had worked as Jon had said it would. It had fooled the Death's Head program into thinking its targets had been killed, making the deadly program run its last command and delete itself.

The gunshot wound to her calf, although clean, hurt like hell. Orchid wiped the bile from her mouth and hobbled over to where Norton lay. He was still curled up in a ball with his back facing her. She looked over to Royal who lay motionless. His face, twisted with fear, held lifeless eyes that looked back at her in a putrid pool of his own juices. A mixture of blood and vomit.

'Norton?' Orchid nudged him on the shoulder, hoping to get a response.

Norton held a thumbs up to her and slowly rolled over. He looked at her with a pained expression on his face.

'Are you okay?' she asked.

He looked into her eyes with a deadpan expression and said, 'I think I've shit myself.'

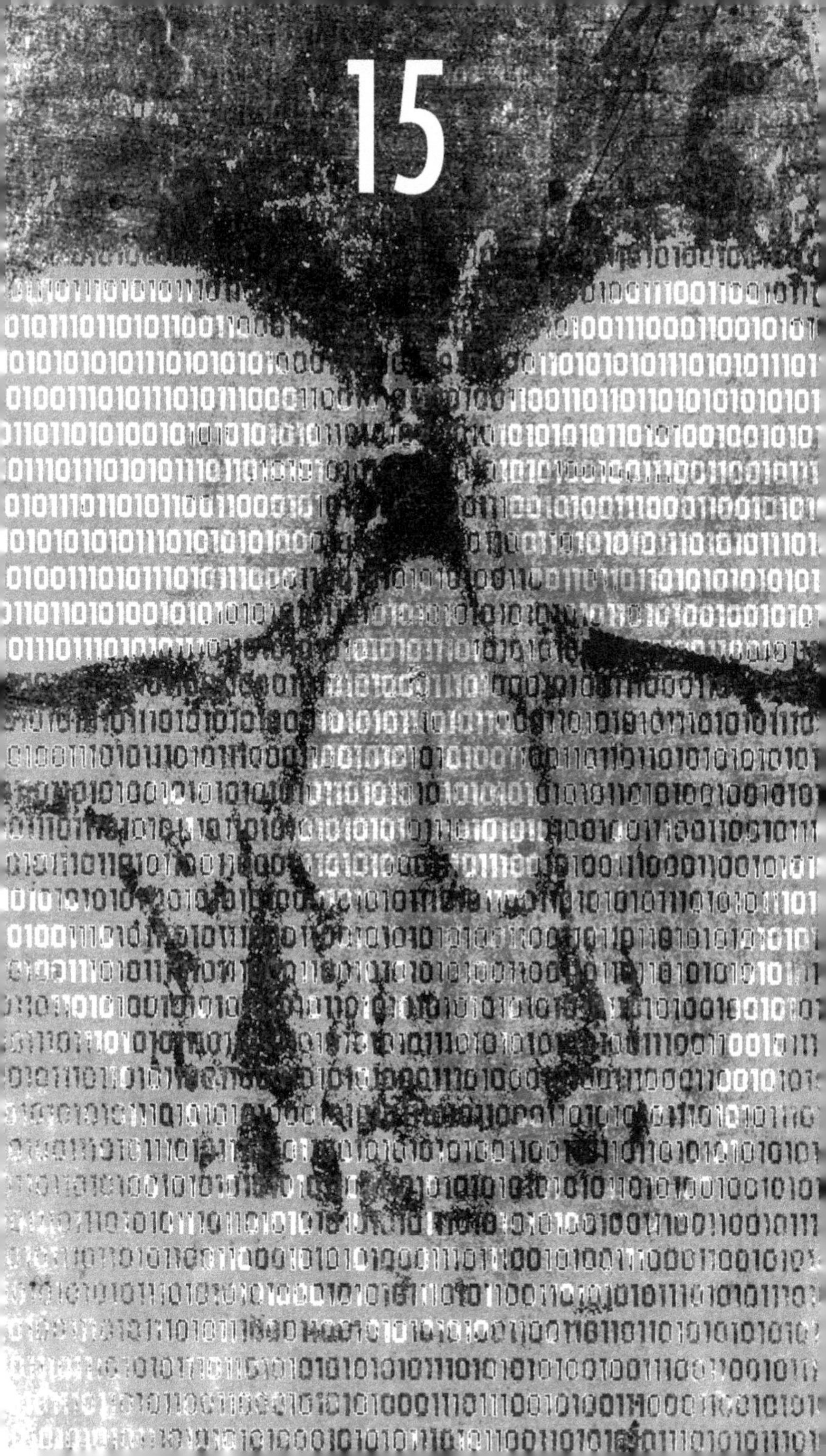
15

The day was characteristically grey as Norton walked out of the police station and headed to his car. His face was bruised and scabby, his wounds were bandaged underneath his suit. The last few days had cruelly punished his body. The wind picked up as he made his way across the car park and blew a gentle, soothing gust across his face. He closed his eyes and let the breeze bring him a much needed freshness before he stepped into his car. He didn't drive off straight away but sat back to watch the pedestrians strolling along, the traffic zooming by, people going about their business.

'So they believe you then?' Orchid's silky tones startled the detective and he rose from his introspection.

She was sat in the back seat, but Norton did not turn around, he did not look directly at her.

'It's a long and complicated story but the Chief Inspector believes me enough not to fire me,' he replied, keeping his eyes fixed on the view through his windscreen. 'He isn't going to investigate, he knows it will do no good. The back up files of the room scan shows that my finger prints weren't originally at the scene of the crime, and neither was a gas canister.'

'Saved by computers,' Orchid joked.

'I think he's going back to the notebook,' Norton retorted.

The two laughed together.

When the laughter died down Orchid spoke with a half serious, half playful tone, 'I suppose you should arrest me.'

'Not today Orchid, I'm off duty,' he sounded relaxed and gave a deep sigh. 'I've been given a couple of weeks off.'

'Good you need it,' Orchid sympathized with him. She opened the door to leave but before she did she had one last thing to say, 'Thanks for helping out, but listen, I don't ever want to see you again. You're bad for business.'

With that Orchid shut the door and walked away. Norton didn't look back to watch her leave, instead he kept his eyes focused forward. A mother and daughter walked down the street. The child was excitedly telling her mother the wonderful things that had happened at school today. Norton smiled. He would take a couple of weeks off. He needed time to grieve.

The world could turn without him.
Around him.
He needed to bleed for a while.
To feel the pain and accept it.

But at least the world was a safer place, whatever he did,

or didn't, know.

His mobile rang as he watched the young girl jumping in puddles. The child shrieked with excited and unbridled joy as she came crashing down into the water, soaking herself. Norton reached down to his phone and put it to his ear.

Had he looked at the screen he would have noticed the name of the caller.

Mel.

ABOUT THE AUTHOR

J. R. Park stopped writing when he left university and
didn't start again until over ten years later. He has
always had a love for all things horror and although he
can't change a tyre on a car he can tell you the full
history of Italian zombie cinema.
He currently lives in Bristol, in similar conditions as a
student, which is probably not very becoming for a man
of his age.

PUNCH – J. R. PARK

It's carnival night in the seaside town of Stanswick Sands
and tonight blood will stain the beach red.
Punch and Judy man, Martin Powell, returns after ten
years with a dark secret. As his past is revealed Martin
must face the anger of the hostile townsfolk, pushing
him to the very edge of sanity.
Humiliated and stripped of everything he holds dear,
Martin embarks on a campaign of murderous revenge,
seeking to settle scores both old and new.

The police force of this once sleepy town can't react
quick enough as they watch the body count grow at the
hands of a costumed killer.
Can they do enough to halt the malicious mayhem of the
twisted Punch?

PUNCH

J. R. Park

"It's a heartbreaking tale. I'd strongly urge anyone, looking for a straight forward raw read to buy this as soon as possible."
DK Ryan, author of Egor The Rat & creator of HorrorWorlds.com

"Graphical nightmares effectively place the reader in an uneasy position."
Horror Palace

"A rousing combo of parental angst and seething evil. A great spin on the post-modern serial killer."
Daniel Marc Chant, author of Burning House

"A hard hitting story of the darker side of life in a sleepy little seaside town."
Paul Pritchard, Amazon reviewer

UPON WAKING – J. R. PARK

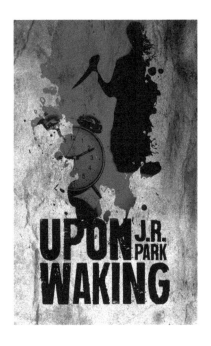

What woke you from your sleep?
Was it the light coming through the curtains? The traffic
from the street outside?

Or was it the scratching through the walls? The cries of
tormented anguish from behind locked doors? The
desperate clawing at the woodwork from a soul hell bent
on escape?

Welcome to a place where the lucky ones die quickly.

Upon waking, the nightmare truly begins.

"It's basically like John Doe's murderous fantasies in
Se7en with Clive Barker dancing naked on top of it."
Daniel Marc Chant, author of Maldicion & Burning
House

"Sick. Demands a re-read."
Duncan P. Bradshaw, author of Class Three

"Such vivid images. J. R. Park is a sick man." – Mistress
Fi, fetish model

For up to date information on the work of J. R. Park
visit:

JRPark.co.uk
Facebook.com/JRParkAuthor
Twitter @Mr_JRPark

For further information on the Sinister Horror
Company visit:

SinisterHorrorCompany.com
Facebook.com/sinisterhorrorcompany
Twitter @SinisterHC

Lightning Source UK Ltd.
Milton Keynes UK
UKHW01f1819220918
329363UK00001B/6/P